About the Author

Ruth Hartley is an artist and independent author of novels, essays and poems. She has a BA (Arts) and an MA (Women's Studies). Born in Zimbabwe, educated in South Africa, exiled in London from 1966, she worked for over 20 years in Zambia as artist and Director of an art gallery and later in Cambridge as an artist. Now living in France, Ruth Hartley is working on her fourth novel.

Also by the Author

The Shaping of Water (2014) Against the backdrop of Lake Kariba and the Liberation Wars, personal and environmental damage and displacement cause dreams to founder on the rocks of political reality. As different families fight to keep their ideals alive, they find themselves connected in unexpected ways.

The Tin Heart Gold Mine (2017) For centuries European wars have impacted on Africa and the world. Lara, a wildlife artist, learns from Oscar, entrepreneur and survivor, how art can be an instrument of war and from Tim, a journalist, that truth is important. What is truth and who is the father of her child ?

The Love and Wisdom Crimes (2019) A coming of age adventure story about a young white woman who discovers that, in apartheid South Africa, it is dangerous to love a revolutionary and a crime to love someone black.

Poems from the Spiral-Bound Notebooks (2019) The poems from Southern Africa that inspired 'The Love and Wisdom Crimes'.

When I Was Bad : a Memoir (2019) Ruth Hartley recounts her first year in London as an exile and unmarried mother of a mixed-race child in the Swinging Sixties.

www.ruthhartley.com

WHEN WE WERE WICKED

RUTH HARTLEY

atypical
BOOKS

atypical books
47, Route des Pyrénées,
65700 Labatut-Rivière,
France
Tel: 00 33 562 37 53 08
Email: ruth@ruthhartley.com
Web: ruthhartley.com
Twitter: @ruthhartley9

ISBN 978 2955734 445

British Library Cataloguing in Publication Data.
A catalogue record for this book is available from the British Library.

Typeset in 11pt Aldine401 by Troubador Publishing Ltd, Leicester, UK

Matador is an imprint of Troubador Publishing Ltd

For my mother, Pixie

Contents

Sinners and saints, villains and heroes,
the children, women and men in these stories
all find ways to survive in wicked times.

Some of these stories are old and were
written down decades ago.
Some are new.

Some of these stories make me laugh.
Some stories were inspired by my ill-spent youth.
Some are wicked inventions.

Two are short memoirs about wicked people.
I fell over them so often in dark dreams that I was
forced to dig them out of the sludge of my memory
and expose them to light.

"I was so much older then, when I was young."
- as Eric Burdon and the Animals sang in 1967

Not in Front of the Children
A Memoir

Every fourth Sunday after church Mum drove us to Chikurubi
prison.

I didn't know why we had to wait outside it in the car. I didn't
know it was a prison. Neither did my sister. I was five. She was
three. I knew black people went to prison. I didn't know that
white people did.

Chikurubi Prison stood in the middle of nowhere, a flat-
walled, introverted fortress with guns pointing into its own guts.
Its brick bulk was too solid to ignore and too dull to remember.
Mum drove there in silence. She parked on the dirt forecourt,
wound the windows almost shut, got out and locked us inside.

"I won't be long," she said, a small crease between her
eyebrows. The bright sun was hard on her face. She turned
away and disappeared through a small opening in a huge
double gate.

Around us the flattened valley was cleared of trees and its grass
cut short to a stiff ankle-scratching yellow-brown length. The
heavy, hazy midday sun pressed down on the stifling car while
around it cicadas shrilled like boiling kettles. We may have sweated
and squabbled in our Sunday School clothes, but I remember
succumbing to lethargy and sleep rather than fractiousness. Mum
was always gone exactly half an hour, after which we went home
to roast meat prepared by our African cook and carved by our
frowning father while Mum smiled and smiled. This strange gap

in our Sunday was never commented on and had no connection at all with the rest of our lives.

My sister and I often squabbled, but Uncle Bruce's first appearance in our home a year earlier occasioned one of our fiercest and most physical fights. Bruce was Mum's younger brother, a bespectacled adult in the body of an underfed adolescent. We didn't notice his height because we were even smaller. Despite his minimal size, Uncle Bruce managed to smuggle a ginger tom-kitten right past our watching parents. It was a gift that didn't divide in two. Skilled parenting prevented the kitten's early demise and us from suffering terrible lacerations. We still fell on each other over its name until Mum recombined our opposed choices of Jackson and Peter, suggested by the brand of cigarettes in Bruce's shirt pocket. Peter Jackson, the tobacco-coloured kitten, remained a thorny problem. Kidnapped by Bruce from a feral cat family, he soon effected his escape. I don't think my sister and I minded much. Peter Jackson was hard to catch and impossible to cuddle.

Uncle Bruce visited at weekends, bringing other gifts. While he was with us, the grown-ups said little to each other and told us off more than usual. Once he brought some surprisingly gorgeous doll's clothes. Mummy, calm as ever, asked him where he "found" them, then quietly put them away "just to keep them safe".

After that there was the tennis match. On Saturdays the grown-ups played at the club across the road. One dramatic afternoon, Uncle Bruce came racing back into the kitchen to bathe his face under the kitchen tap. His opponent had smashed the tennis ball into Bruce's face and he had glass splinters around his eyes from his spectacles. Who, I wonder, had decided to aim such a hard shot at his head?

One evening Uncle Bruce and a "friend" without a name, came to ask Dad for help. They had "lost" the keys to their digs and needed to get in through a window. As there was no baby-sitter, we all squeezed into the car, a ladder was secured on top and Dad drove us to the "wrong" part of town behind Salisbury Kopje. It was full of rustling, shifting shapes as the sky darkened. Mum, Dad, my sister and I watched as Uncle Bruce and his friend leaned the ladder against the side of the house, forced entry and climbed in.

"Do they live there?" Mum asked with a reassuring smile at us.

"They're breaking in," Dad said, with irony but no smile.

Uncle Bruce came out of the house alone and carried the ladder back to the car.

The next time Uncle Bruce came by, my sister and I were half-conscious and too ill to scratch our measles pustules. He promised to babysit whilst Mum went to the chemist for medicine. When she returned we were alone. Uncle Bruce had been through the bedroom cupboards, found Dad's illegal pistol, a souvenir from his war service, pocketed it and disappeared.

As soon as my sister and I recovered from the measles we were separated and sent away to live with other families. It must have been January 1949 because that month I went to school in a crowded class of fifty children and an indifferent "auntie" took me there, not my kind Mum. It was a time soon after the end of the Second World War when soldiers and airmen were returning home to the settler colony of Rhodesia with new wives, and families from all over Europe were arriving in search of a better life. It was a time of enormous division and inequality between Africans and Europeans.

We returned home many weeks later in a state of shocked alienation to find that Granny Emma had come to live with us. Mum and Uncle Bruce were her children. Dad had built her a small round room with a grass roof behind our house. Granny Emma smelt of the camphor wood wedding chest in which she still stored her clothes. She crocheted all the time making doilies, tea cosies, and covers for toilet paper rolls. When Granny Emma was surprised or amused, she hooted like an owl. My sister and I found her fascinating. Dad found her annoying.

"Your Granny deserves respect!" Mum explained with a smile. "Her family were very poor German settlers. She grew up without shoes and had to leave school at fourteen."

3

Granny Emma found a job in another small town and went to work there. She was saving all her money for her special dream.

"I want to go around the world," she said, and her bosom heaved with a soundless hoot.

We didn't think that was possible, but when Granny Emma retired in her 60s, she did go around the world. It took her a year. She travelled by boat and train without leaving the British Empire. Afterwards she wrote blue aerogramme letters of affection in her childish scrawl to new and younger penfriends.

"Woohooh!" Granny Emma hooted when I made a drawing. "You're artistic! Just like Bruce!"

I wasn't sure I wanted to be linked to my uncle. By the time I was nine, I knew he was in prison, though not why. Besides, the proof of Uncle Bruce's artistry was a charming little story book he had made about my pretty sister and I was jealous.

Bruce painted a shop sign for my mother's farm store. It showed a queue of unsmiling Africans waiting for it to open. There was no sunshine in the painting, nor, I guess, in the prison workshop where Uncle Bruce was being rehabilitated ready for his release and deportation. He had one whole year to wait. I was thirteen by then and at boarding school. It was judged I was old enough to hear some of the truth. I sat down in my uniform on a school chair while Mum told me about her brother. Uncle Bruce was a South African-born criminal who had served his time. The police would escort him on the train to the Rhodesian border then she would travel with him to a Christian organisation that would help him find work in a country he no longer knew.

I was allowed to go to the railway station to say goodbye to my mother. I wouldn't see Uncle Bruce. She stood rigid and still, looking straight ahead until the stationmaster informed her Uncle Bruce was on board and under police guard, then she turned, kissed me and climbed stiffly onto the train. We waved goodbye through clouds of steam.

My mother's brother was a double murderer. That awful knowledge was a bloated secret inside me. I had to tell someone about, it but who? What would happen when I did? I would burst if I didn't. I was too young to know that it was only a secret for me and my sister. It was not a secret to anyone else in Rhodesian society.

"A nine-day wonder only!" the newspaper editor had said when my Dad asked him not to print the story of Bruce's capture and trial. "I have to run it. People will forget soon enough."

Did they? Was the story of Bruce's release ten years later also covered in the newspapers?

Mum was pale and tired after her train trip with Uncle Bruce.

"I don't know how he did it. As soon as the police left us at the border, Bruce got drunk. Somehow he bribed the restaurant-car staff to give him alcohol."

My mother, nevertheless, manoeuvred her intoxicated brother across Johannesburg and down to Pietermaritzburg.

Uncle Bruce was wild and high when we next saw him.

"I'm not drinking! I won't drink!" he kept stating, but he couldn't stand or sit still for one moment. We had stopped by to see how Uncle Bruce was doing on our journey to a long-promised seaside holiday.

At the last moment Dad refused to come with us.

"I'm retired now," he said. "We can't afford a holiday!"

"I've resigned," he wrote to his office.

"You're sacked," his boss replied.

The friend that Dad, in his role as General Secretary of the Grain Marketing Board, had employed as an accountant had embezzled funds. I don't suppose it helped that Dad's brother-in-law was a murderer. We didn't get any stolen money, whatever the case.

Mummy's smiles no longer had the power to sooth Dad. He wanted Mummy, my sister and me to understand that he really was a good person. We had to keep telling him it was true and that we knew it for a fact.

My parents were divorced the following year.

My sad and bitter Dad said it was all the fault of Granny Emma.

"Emma spoilt Bruce. Emma spoilt your mother. Your mother is wilful – unreasonable."

Poor Dad. He set out to find a new wife who would spoil him.

Eventually I asked Mum what Bruce had really done and she told me the story in bits and pieces whenever we were alone. My new stepfather, Jack, had enough of war. He had served in the Far East where he had been reported "missing, believed killed". Now he was focussed on paying back the Land Bank loan for the few acres of tobacco he could grow among the rocks and *vleis* of the surrounding bush. He had no time to indulge female feelings. Sometimes Mummy didn't smile.

"Bruce was a wild boy. . . it was the Second World War . . . at sixteen, he enlisted in the South African Army and was sent to Italy . . . too young to bear arms, he became a Dispatch Rider carrying messages between the British front lines. It was very dangerous work . . . Bruce was Mentioned In Dispatches for his bravery but as always, he was out of control . . . he got into a fight, had a duel with another soldier and shot and killed him. . . too young to be executed by a firing-squad after the court-martial, Bruce was brought back in chains to a South African prison. Conditions were so terrible he lost his teeth and became very ill."

"Granny Emma never gave up on Bruce . . . she began a long campaign to get him pardoned on account of his youth and bravery . . . finally she saw General Jan Smuts who did pardon Bruce . . . that is how he was able to come to live near us in Rhodesia."

"My father was an alcoholic. Granny Emma was forced to leave him," Mum added. "It must have affected Bruce."

For almost four years Bruce wasn't mentioned in my hearing. There were other heavy drinkers in the family. Pregnancy and madness became the current family problems, not murder.

Then it was Christmas Eve and suicide time. We were gathered together in the farmhouse sitting-room, Mum, Granny Emma, my sister, my stepfather, Jack, and his two young daughters. We had eaten. That quiet moment of fullness and contentment was shattered when the phone rang in the passage.

No other telephone sounds like an old country phone. Ours was a wall-mounted, black metal box with brass hooks to hold the receiver, a stiff noisy dial, and a crank-handle at its side. All the local white farmers shared the same exchange. Three turns of the crank handle, three rings and anyone could pick it up. More rings and it was the central exchange calling. If it rang it was either gossip or very important. We always jumped up and answered at once. Christmas is also the season of thunderstorms and interference on the phone line. We heard crackling and shouting. My sister came back her voice high-pitched in panic.

"I can't hear! It's from South Africa!"

Mum took over. The crackling and the distant thunder increased in volume but those of us left in the sitting room heard her repeat odd words in her clear voice.

"BRUCE."

"DEAD."

"CAR." Or was it "CARBON MONOXIDE."?

"SUICIDE."

My stepfather stood up and marched out to the passage.

"IT'S CHRISTMAS EVE! I DO NOT WANT TO HEAR ANOTHER WORD ON THIS SUBJECT."

He slammed down the phone. We heard everything he said. We did not speak a word.

Granny Emma was absolutely still. Her expression did not alter at all. For the rest of Christmas, I couldn't look anyone in the face. No one mentioned Bruce. My grandmother's pain and my

7

stepfather's cruelty were the most extreme I had yet witnessed. Forty years afterwards when Steve, my own Dad, was alone for the second time and rational once more, he was told me about Bruce's crime and trial.

"Bruce was out of work, on drink and drugs. He burgled a house, broke his parole terms, and was to be sent back to prison in South Africa. He had no plans, but finding my gun made him decide to make a run for the border, get secretly into South Africa and avoid jail. He found a taxi to take him to the border. When the African taxi-driver ran out of petrol and money Bruce shot him dead and hid his body in the boot. Why, we will never know. There was already a manhunt in progress. Soon afterwards the police caught up with Bruce and arrested him."

The trial was a scandal. The uproar decided my parents to send us away from home even though I was to start school for the first time.

"At the trial Bruce conducted his own defence," my father said, "He appeared to be a skinny little white man who had got into an argument with an African and been forced to fight for his life. He was in fact, tough and very strong for his size."

Racism must have played a part in the jury's verdict. The judge, Sir Robert Clarkson Tredgold, found Bruce guilty of culpable homicide and sentenced him to ten years. His previous court martial and convictions had not been admissible in court, but when they were read out later, Tredgold was shocked. Did Bruce deserve to escape the death sentence? It was an injustice for the taxi-driver and his family. I never knew what my mother and grandmother felt about any of it. I only know what they did. I know that Bruce's life changed all of ours. When I tried to find out the facts about the murdered taxi driver from the Zimbabwe Archive in 1980, I was refused help. It was a sensitive time politically and a sensitive matter racially.

At my mother's funeral, I spoke of her love and her courage as well as her silent acceptance of hardship.

"Mum's life was sometimes tragic," I said. "Her brother committed suicide – probably the result of Post-Traumatic Stress Disorder after the war."

"Oh, of course!" my cousins said, "We never really knew – we weren't told."

Was Bruce damaged, mad, or simply bad? Did I speak the truth?

In the rainy season in Africa, the caterpillars of the moth Pachymeta Robusta, the Msasa worm, grow to an impressive size. They are covered with stiff, black and orange, prickly hairs an inch long. Touching them causes painful blisters and a terrible itching that's quite dangerous for a child. While the excitement of Bruce's 1949 trial infected every household in the country, I was five years old, in the temporary care of my "auntie" and I knew nothing of it. During those first days at school, I sat lost and alone, in my new school uniform made two sizes too large for me by my careful mother. It was just loose enough for two boys to drop a couple of giant hairy caterpillars down my back. The fierce prickling began at once. I stood up, turned awkwardly and saw two flailing fiery creatures fall away from under my skirt. My "auntie" collected me from school and put me into a tepid bath of bicarbonate of soda for a whole day.

It is only recently that I've connected that childhood experience with my destructive and tortured Uncle Bruce and what some parents may have gossiped about in front of their children.

Pictures at an Exhibition

JANINE

Eight o'clock already! Thank God! Not long to go now -
  God! How I hate all this. I must have been given about ten
different glasses of wine and I don't know what happened to any
of them. I don't think I drank any of them but I feel pissed or – do
I just feel sick?
  "Yes please. I'd love one! Definitely, I need it. Thanks!"
  There are so many people here I don't know -
I think I don't know.
  "Hello Annie. Great to see you! Glad you like it. Thanks. Thanks."
  I can't believe that it's nearly over.
  I can't believe that I finished all these paintings in time. Oh
God – that one's still wet! Please don't touch it lady – whoever
you are! Oh God! It's the woman who collects my raptor series.
She almost got the entire lot, from a lizard buzzard to a martial
eagle. She won't like that new one at all. I'll look away.
  "Thanks – no, dry wine is just what I like. Thanks."
  Keep smiling and looking as if I am part of Frankie's group.
  *"Oh yes – different direction in my painting – yes – thanks. Oh sorry
– you prefer my old work? Sorry."*
  *"Thanks. Yes – oh, you like this new stuff? Yes – well I guess it's not
so easy to live with as the elephant at sunset."*
  Oh shit! Why do I paint? It's certainly not to exhibit it and
get all this pain! Okay it brings in the money – or at least my old-

style paintings do – or is that "did"? Frankie did warn me when I showed him my new work. In fact, he warned me over and over.

"Janine, sweetheart," he said. *"This stuff is very exciting my darling, but it won't sell easily. Really, my love. Your customers will just hate it. All these years you've been selling them a special dream about the beauty of the wild and now you are going to hit them with the fact that it's dying and they're killing it."*

Frankie kept shaking his head and looking from me to my new paintings and back again.

"Janine, my sweetheart. This is good this new work – but tough. You're challenging us, my darling. Can you bear to be hated? And –"

Frankie stopped with two dramatic gestures. One to the left and one to the right.

"How can I make one exhibition from this new work here – and this old stuff here – together? It won't work, you know. The people who'll buy your new work will make your regulars feel just a little past it. Not good, my love. Mmm-mmhnn!"

Then he gave me the same thorough scrutiny that he had just given the paintings.

"Yes, Janine," he said. *"What about that beautiful tanned boy you are married to? Is he going to let you run wild with your new work? Will he swap a goldmine wife who paints wildlife for a real artist who is famous but can't sell her work?"*

Frankie adores talking about love and sex and art. As for me, I haven't talked to Rick about my new work. We have hardly had time to talk to each other this past season. He has been busy filming with Sabrina and I have been busy painting for this show.

Frankie makes out that he fancies Rick. As for me, I love Rick. He is everything to me and has been since we were at school. We have been so happy in our life alone together in the bush. I don't paint to change my life. I paint because my paintings insist that I make them as they want to be. These last paintings have been so extremely demanding that at times I felt almost possessed. Not that I told Rick, of course. I did tell Sabrina though. Talking to her has been good. She is so creative herself and she understands why I feel so driven – it is the same for her as for me with our work.

"Frankie! Really! You think the Jo'burg Star art critic likes my new work! You mean it! That's fantastic! Perhaps the sales will get better then?"

Where is Rick, actually? I keep seeing him across the other side of the room. It's pretty crowded in here but it's not like him not to be closer to me some of the time. Last night was such a rush getting the last paintings signed and hung that I didn't see him at all. He was asleep when I got home. Oh, there he is! He looks as tired as I feel. I'll send him a telepathic message.

"Rick! Rick! Come over here if you can please?"

Sabrina has already made a special point of coming over to kiss me and say how good the work looks displayed properly. She has been a great support and encouragement, but then Sabrina is so sorted out. She really does know what she wants from life and how to get it. I will miss her terribly when she and the film crew go back to London and we go back to just being Rick and Janine.

Why doesn't Rick come and find me?

SABRINA

Good! This function will wind down soon. I need to get some sleep before the team packs up and we hit the airport road for home.

This has been quite some year. Hard going but successful. Hooray, Sabrina! This film is going to get you back into the big-time big-time. Pat yourself on the back, girl!

That most recent footage we shot about the poachers is so exciting. I can't wait to get into the editing suite to start putting it all together. The film and its ideas are all I want to think about. It's difficult to concentrate on this exhibition sufficiently to do it justice. Not that one can see the paintings for the people, mind. It is bloody crowded and hot in here. Still it is selling, which is good for Rick and Janine. The film will bring in funding for them when it is finally screened but right now they need money from Janine's exhibition.

Janine's a good kid. Funny that I feel older than her when we are the same age. Cynicism is so ageing, ha ha! Or is it just that I have had to fight so hard to do what I want and she hasn't – yet! Janine is very talented but so what? Talent alone is useless? Except that I think Janine *has* got what it takes. I recognise that absorbed look of someone driven by their 'vocation'. Good word 'vocation' as long as you don't claim you have one yourself. Set yourself up as 'having a calling' and someone will knock you down. Say "I only do it for money" and they relax.

I don't think Rick really wants Janine to devote more time to painting than she does to him. Husbands do cramp a girl's ambitions! Don't I know it! Still, I'm a fast learner any road so it doesn't matter. I really enjoyed having Janine for company and she has been useful too. She showed me a whole different side of life for women in the villages. All information I couldn't have found out even from a guy like Rick. It'll give a special new insight to this particular wildlife film – this particular film of mine. Polish your laurels, girl!

Actually, Rick makes this film work. He's a star when it comes to knowledge of game. And he is damn good-looking. That quiet manner. That engaging grin. Those distant-seeing eyes that only outdoor people have. What is it about these men who live in the bush that gets to me? Mmmmm – I think about the nape of his sunburnt neck and smell of sun-dried sweat on his khaki shirt and I want to press my face between his shoulder blades and put my arms down – well – . Then I start to think of how smoothly his hips connect with his perky little bum – yes – weeeell!

That wasn't such a good idea. Too many hot nights in the bush – it's bad for me. But it was delicious and not serious. I made that clear. Rick said he understood. I feel a bitch about Janine though – I wasn't really planning it. In fact, Rick and me have had some pretty mean arguments lately. I guess that that winds you up and confrontation can add that edge to sex – or maybe sex is why one gets into confrontation! Those *are* the ambivalences you enjoy – don't you, Sabrina?

Strange, but it's Janine I really care about. Not that we'll see much of each other again, but I will miss her. There will be other guys with tight bums, but fewer artists who are friends like Janine. Rick really thinks there is only space in marriage for one person to have a vocation and it goes without saying that saving wild animals is it and not making art or films!

Right! Time to circulate.

"Hello Frankie darling – what a fantastic show you've put on for Janine! All those red stickers – wow – isn't that something! No. I don't know where darling Ricky is Frankie – he's keeping an even lower profile here than he does in the bush."

Janine is wilting a bit and let's face it Frankie's brilliant at putting up exhibitions and selling art, but he's exhausting company. I think I'll buy another small painting to go with the first one I chose. Rick looks pretty tense too. He seems angry with Janine rather than scared she'll find out about our fling. Weird! You would think that it was Janine and me who had been unfaithful to him. Now that is an interesting thought – what is *that* all about?

RICK

Jeez man! How much longer do we have to hang around here? I just do not enjoy cocktail parties and previews. This is not what I want to do or where I want to be. I do it for Janine, of course. Well, perhaps that's not fair. She doesn't exactly enjoy her shows either. It's the painting she loves. It's beginning to really hack me off that she spends so much of her time doing it. I know she doesn't skimp on her share of the camp work, but its kind of – frustrating.

I don't know exactly what it is she does that annoys me so much – she seems to be in a dream sometimes. Her own private world. It's not fair. So far, we have shared everything. The book I wrote about poaching – this film that Sabrina's been making. It's the art Janine keeps to herself.

I know she's good. I liked her old paintings. They fitted well in with what we do. Looked good in my book. These new ones though – they're disturbing. I can see that it's about the poachers – about the bush – about the villagers – even about the tourists – but it's not going to help making art like this.

That bloody over-the-top queen Frankie is encouraging her. He is giving her ideas. How can Janine be a successful artist in Jo'burg when she lives in the bush with me? I need her. I do. The camp needs her. The project needs her. She can't do this kind of stuff. I'll tell her tomorrow. As soon as Sabrina's gone. I'll tell Janine that it's just not on. Just not on! When Sabrina's gone.

"Ja. Frank – er – Frankie! I'll join you just now man."

When you stop talking to Sabrina maybe. Why does he look at me like that?

Jeezus man! Did Sabrina and me really – do it, – make love – um, – screw last night? God it was great! Having a woman come onto you like that! It takes the guilt out of it. She's a pretty terrific woman as well. Stylish, very sexy, strong – bloody bossy for a woman. She really knows what she wants. And she goes and gets it too. And she wanted me! Jeezus Christ! I was late getting home, though.

It's Janine's fault really -

Well, that's not fair, but she has been so busy with painting for this exhibition. Then last night – having to do that last-minute signing and finishing off and spending so long with Frankie. What does she expect? I'm only human and it wasn't my idea. I was pretty bitter with Sabrina so it's funny it ended up with us in bed. These last few weeks getting the filming finished, packing up camp, Janine working non-stop. It was argument after argument. Both women were really getting me down. The film and the paintings are – just – not – as important – as – stopping the poaching! It was better when there was just Janine and me.

16

She used to make me feel that what I do matters – that I'm good at it!

Sabrina says my work is important but she also – well – always asking why and what and being critical. Why don't they seem to see that tonight? Sabrina is the one who really started Janine on all this new work by talking about the latest films in London, the latest art in London. Where does it lead to? Okay. I'm not as articulate as Sabrina except in my field but I know that Janine's painting is getting too serious and it's not good for us. Janine has got to see that it's not fair to me, her working so hard and so long at – *art!*

Janine has got to see that if she carries on like this, I will end up sleeping with other women. Perhaps if she knew about me and Sabrina she would come to her senses. Sabrina made me promise though. God! It would feel good if everyone in this room knew I had made it with a woman like Sabrina. If I stand near her would everyone suss us out?

God! It would be terrible if Janine found out! What would she do? I love her so much! I really, really love her so much. I can't bear to be without her. She must stay all mine. I can *not* share her with anyone – *or anything!* It's not fair of her to expect me to.

Actually, Janine's looking pretty tired and white and I am sick of drinking this cheap Stein. One glass is enough to sicken you and I've had plenty-plenty! Sabrina is driving us home and it's our last night together.

Just the three of us!

Horse

"It's cruel! It's wrong!"

Sarah is defiant.

She looks at Horse. Horse looks back. Two stubborn beasts with brown, black-lashed eyes. Sarah's face is round like her spectacles. Horse's belly is round from lack of exercise. Pat can school Horse on the lunge line but she will not be able to persuade her daughter to change her mind.

"We can't keep him if you don't ride him," Pat says, reasonably.

"He's mine." Sarah is marginally less strident, also reasonable.

"You gave him to me. I decide what happens to him."

Adopting the impossible role of the loving realist, Pat says, "Yes, honey, but you don't pay for food, livery or vet bills."

Sarah is adamant.

"I don't want him to be ridden by anyone at all – ever! It's cruel to make an animal do the will of a human!"

Horse stands still. Pat sighs and leans harder on Horse. She leans on his left shoulder, one hand on his soft nose, her forehead against the hard curve of his muscled neck. She breathes in the animal heat of Horse, the edible vegetable smell of dung and urine on straw bedding. Herbivorous Horse smells better than carnivorous Cat and omnivorous Dog. Sarah hasn't yet demanded that Pat doesn't stroke Cat or walk Dog, but then neither pet obeys Pat's will. Pat averts her gaze from Cat and Dog when Sarah is at home. She feeds them in secret just in case they too have to be

19

returned to Nature or the Animal Refuge via the wilderness of the Village High Street.

Grungy human vegetarians don't smell as good as Horse. They are smoked not groomed. Sarah has become a vegetarian and on Sunday nights smells of grunge instead of manure and riding boots. At first it was just hunting that was cruel but now it is riding Horse, or any horse at all. Sarah's grungy dread-locked boyfriend doesn't come to the stables even when Sarah is there alone. The Pony Club trophies and rosettes have gone from Sarah's bedroom shelf to shoe boxes in her cupboard though not yet to the dustbin. Grungy Boy a.k.a. 'Sky' has taken Sarah's virginity but not yet all her pride or determination. Pat is hopeful. Sky is making successful inroads on Sarah's mind and individuality. Pat despairs.

There is a deadly war going on. A war of morality that only the Righteous can win.

Sky the Grungy Boy is battling with Horse for the soul of Sarah.

Pat tells herself that it can't be her battle. Her maternal relationship is mere collateral damage. She can take her injuries to the Tack Room and the brandy hidden in the First Aid Box. Horse must fight his own battle.

It is an unequal battle and Horse will lose.

Horse will lose the battle but Pat will be a casualty too.

"Horse is your horse," says Pat with decision. This is true but Pat loves Horse more than she can admit. Pat must not be seen by Sarah as her rival for Horse. She hands the reins to her reluctant daughter,

"If you won't ride him and you won't let him be ridden by anyone here – not even me – then he must be sold. Here – take him and see that he is groomed, check his shoes and feet – Jane is bringing Elspeth round – they may buy him."

"I don't want him to be ridden." Sarah's voice is smaller, her lip quivers. The pain of losing Horse is unbearable for her. Pat turns her head away at the sight. She must sit firm. Harden the heart that lost a stirrup at Sarah's grief.

"He's too young to be put out to grass," Pat says, "He needs exercise or his health will suffer and he can't run wild. Be sensible Sarah. How can I tell someone who buys him what they can do with him? You can't give him away – he's too valuable!" She feels a small mean triumph, a tiny hope, some doubt at Sarah's next materialist demand.

"You gave him to me so the money is mine."

"Sarah, you know how much Horse costs to keep! Remember the deal – if you were to go to university – or have a gap year –"

Sarah is not going anywhere that takes her away from Sky and says so again, and then again for emphasis.

"Why don't you listen, Mum? I will not join global capitalist exploiters!"

Pat remembers that her darling child experimented with chewing while she was being breastfed. Pat bites back.

"You won't want the money then, will you?"

She thinks bitterly that the money would only go on a yurt or a tipi for Sky. And what would tent-dwelling, horse-riding nomads think of Sarah's definition of riding as gratuitous and unnecessary cruelty? Pat mutters to herself then sighs. All arguments and persuasions have been tried and failed. Horse is not going to the fields of Paradise or any Happy Hunting Ground, Horse is going to be gone – no more – and finally together with all horses that have no use and are never ridden he will become extinct.

"What you don't use – you lose!" She had tried to say something like that to Sarah. Sarah had thought that Pat meant it as a threat to Sarah but the threat was to Horse.

"What will you do with the money?" Sarah asks aggressively.

"I suppose," replies Pat with sadness, "that I will get rid of Donkey at the same time. He has needed to be replaced for ages."

"Why?" Sarah is surprised into asking.

"I could use a better quality of transport."

Pat doesn't really want technology, she likes animals. She wants her feet on the ground and her spade in horse manure.

"You, Mum! A new car – instead of Donkey?" Sarah is shocked.

"We got Donkey because of Horse and for Horse, remember? I won't need a beaten-up old van with a faulty heater and windscreen wiper if we don't have to transport feed for Horse."

"I won't buy a new car, but I will buy as green a car as I can." Pat adds, quickly, before Sarah can criticise.

Mother and Daughter stand between their tame animal past and an uncertain and savage technological future. Sarah holds Horse's leather bridle. Pat holds the metal keys to Donkey.

Horse simply waits.

The Pink Kite

Carole had made a brave start.

She had packed a bright-green, fluffy towel, a bright-turquoise, slick raincoat, and a shiny-pink and gold, romantic novel by a young and fairly avant-garde writer. She hoped that Sarah, her daughter, would be impressed that she was reading something so raunchy. Maybe she would ask to borrow it.

Carole had hesitated a little and then decided against the multi-coloured sweets for Panos. Hard to know what to take him as he would already have a lollipop-red bucket and a yellow spade. She wasn't confident about buying books for him. Sarah looked them over disparagingly because Panos had always read them last year. Carole supposed he found the time to read so many stories because he didn't have a regular bedtime. He always seemed to be flopped on the floor in a tip of toys and books long after the nine o'clock watershed had passed. Sarah was always at the kitchen table having a late supper with a clutter of friends or phoning them up to gossip.

Maybe Carole had triumphed at last and finally chosen the right gift for Panos. A neon-pink plastic kite lay rolled up in her basket, compromised by an adulterous liaison with Carole's discreet bottle-green umbrella.

The purchasing and packaging of the cheerfully coloured new objects had energised her. Powered by the head of steam she had raised, she was propelled from her flat, to a taxi, to the station, and at last, to the York train. Catching her mood exactly, the York train had moved off promptly at the guard's peremptory whistle but now, less than two hours later, the head of steam was entirely dissipated. The train sat silently in the flat Lincolnshire landscape, its occupants as morose as the grey and sunken sky.

"A delay," announced the intercom. "We'll let you know". Then it went very quiet. There were still two connections to be made before Whitby.

Carole had arrived in limbo again.

Her stomach recognised it first and then her throat constricted. Limbo had been her home since Harry had left with his orange-haired secretary. Its dull misery had the familiarity of intimate association. Living in limbo was a stigma that made Carole unwelcome. It was a disability that caused people to avoid her eyes, get up from the table and busy themselves with cups of instant coffee. When Carole ventured into Sarah's flat, she watched her fidget and noticed that suddenly Panos needed supervision while he cleaned his teeth. Even Panos sometimes watched her with caution from behind his junk yard of cars and extra-terrestrials.

Panos, Carole found, possessed healing powers. A smile and hug from him made the day brighten irrepressibly. Carole loved to see her grandson. She longed for Sarah to give her the same quick, complete smile and hug that Panos did, but Sarah blamed her mother for her father's defection. Sarah felt that Harry had dumped her and Panos when his new wife had a baby. This betrayal was painful for an only daughter and Sarah was angry that Carole had not prevented it.

In spite of this, Carole had invited herself to Whitby to join her daughter and grandson and their four friends who shared a cottage there each August. After a positively hot day in April, when there had been a very funny sitcom about divorced mothers and grown-up daughters on the television, Carole had found, to her astonishment, that the normally hostile and snappish telephone receiver remained docile in her hand while Sarah told her about Panos' seventh birthday. After that compliance Carole had decided to risk everything.

"Sarah, if you are off to Whitby again this summer, could I come up and join you all for a night or two? At a bed and breakfast nearby, perhaps?"

Sarah had answered right back. "That's fine Mum. Claire's bloke, Johnnie, has to work mid-week. There'll be space in the cottage"

Very fast Carole said that she would pay her bit. Maybe she could baby-sit for Panos and for Johnnie and Claire's child.

"I'll cook supper," she said, "or pay for a pub lunch."

There was a brief silence while the well-behaved telephone receiver held its breath. Carole visualised Sarah's expression as she realised what had been agreed.

"Whatever, Mum," she said.

It was arranged. Carole vowed she would be the sitcom mum. No grieving, no face-wiping, and no bed-time clock-watching.

The Whitby sea and Carole's hair might be grey but there would be no grey moods.

"So why had the train got stuck in limbo?"

The train pulled in to Whitby only twenty-five minutes late. This was remarkable considering that ever since Middlesbrough it had in tow a heavy wodge of leaky rain-filled cloud. Carole had fought all the way to free the train from its deadening load. She fortified herself with a sandwich that gaped red tomato and an orange can of something undrinkable and sticky. These had to be followed swiftly by a pale gin and tonic and a beige coffee to restore her self-respect. At last her fight paid off. She emerged from the train, turquoise and shiny into light summer drizzle. She was tired, stiff, but calm and cheerful. The train, however, gave a spiteful whistle and then deposited its burden of depression onto the platform alongside Carole's suitcase.

The arrangement was that Carole would find her own way to the Eastcliff house with her suitcase, then, at her leisure, wander out to find everyone either by the pier or in the tea-room.

25

She found the rented house unlocked. Someone's patchwork shoulder bag lay disembowelled on the settee. A Radio Four play performed to an audience of empty milk bottles and cereal boxes. Books, toys and literary magazines proclaimed that Sarah's friends, like her, had sharp minds and confused life styles. Carole inspected the bedrooms. It seemed that she was expected to sleep in Johnnie's sheets as well as his bed, but, though crumpled, they seemed clean and smelt interesting. Carole wiped the loo seat and flushed the bowl before she used it.

Besides Sarah and Panos, Johnnie, his wife Claire and their child, Susanna, there were two other guests, Tim and Jenny. Carole didn't think they were a couple and suspected that Tim carried a torch for Sarah. Carole felt ignorant about how people under thirty-five conducted relationships. Marriage to a man as domineering as Harry had not given her much experience of being a consenting adult.

"Whatever will we talk about tonight at supper?" she wondered in a sudden panic.

Supper was a long time coming. The beach was only abandoned for the pub when a rainstorm gave them no other option. The pub was only abandoned for the house when the children did likewise. The cooking was done by five people, all talking at once, all feeding two children, and all opening wine bottles. At ten o'clock they sat down very sociably together, exchanging histories and laughter. Sarah and Carole recounting for entertainment their different perspectives of child-bearing and child-rearing and finding to their mutual gratification and surprise that, after all, they had a sense of humour in common.

They awoke to steady rain. The children looked so glum that Carole nearly confessed that rain was her personal travelling companion. Sensibly she decided it wasn't fair on Panos. Bad enough to have only one grandmother, worse if she also came from limbo with attendant rain.

"At teatime, Panos," she said, "a strong wind will blow the rain away just so that we can go and fly the pink kite."

At teatime a strong and very disagreeable wind blew right across the kitchen table.

Carole was not expecting it when it first stirred the loose ends of the kitchen paper wrapped round the fish and chips. Everyone had been for a long tramp up the beach to Sandy End and returned home on the train so late that lunch became high tea. The kite had accompanied them but remained coyly in its plastic mackintosh as there had been neither wind nor sun to seduce it. The conversation had circled about in a relaxed way too. At last the rain had stopped and the sun came out and stood high above the town. There was a momentary lull in the conversation. Suddenly Carole felt the dead weight of exhaustion.

"We should have eaten earlier," she said with disingenuous waspishness.

"The children are tired and grumpy. It is not the right way to treat them like that."

There was an immediate silence. Sarah seemed to be choking on a fish bone and Carole realised she had blown it.

"I'm enjoying myself so much," she said apologetically. "Harry is – was – so much better than me at being sociable. I hope I haven't been too boring -"

She was cut short by the fiercest of scowls from Sarah.

"Mum!" said Sarah, pale and breathless. "Mum!"

"Don't! Don't ever, ever start on like that again!"

"You cannot – you cannot behave like that when I am on holiday with my friends. My life is also hard. I don't need you spoiling everything by being a miserable old woman!"

Carole felt as if the day's cold rain had been tipped over her. She wanted to throw back her head and bawl as loudly as Susanna had just done when Panos hit her.

The kitchen was absolutely quiet. Carole knew she must break the silence, but feared that her voice had lost the power to be heard.

"Sarah," she heard herself say, "Sarah. I am sorry – you are quite right I shouldn't have said that – I do love you and Panos – and my misery is – "

"No," she told herself. "Start again."

"Sarah," she said. "I am NOT miserable. My life is working out very nicely at the moment. In fact –"

An inspiration came to her. "I am going to start an Open University degree this September."

Everyone was standing around awkwardly.

Sarah gulped down her fish bone and fled to the bathroom.

Jenny followed with a sympathetic grimace at Carole, "I'll just go and see. You know."

Claire said, "Hey kids! How about that jigsaw puzzle you like. The "Thomas the Tank Engine" one. You know."

Tim said gently. "Sarah'll be okay. You know."

"I think I'll go and fly the kite," said Carole. "Panos, do you want to come?"

Panos gave a huge sigh, world-weary and important.

"No thank you, Gran. I must stay and look after Mum. *You know.*"

Carole found herself tramping up to Sandy End alone with the pink kite in her hand. Tears were damming up behind her sunglasses and she had to surreptitiously scoop them out sideways with her little finger. Soon she was alone on the beach and she allowed herself to cry aloud. It felt strange. Both a pleasant relief and very theatrical.

After a while she stopped to unwrap the kite. If she was going to attempt an Open University degree she ought first to be sure that she was able to fly a kite. Assembling the flimsy plastic and light rods in the stiff offshore breeze wasn't easy. It had a gorgeous long rainbow-coloured tail that flicked away, impatient to be sky-borne. At Carole's first attempt it twisted itself into a vicious spiral, bucked furiously and made a kamikaze dive into the sea.

Then Carole remembered how to fly kites.

She launched it gently but decisively, walking backwards quickly as the string tautened and the kite rose up and up, and up some more. There it was. A beautiful, magical flying fish or a swimming bird, dancing and diving in the currents and eddies of the flowing air. Once Carole had enjoyed fishing with a twirling, glittering spinner, hoping for the sharp strike and tightening line as the fish raced off and joined her to an underwater world. Now she was connected to two, no, to three worlds. Her feet sometimes on the sand, sometimes in the cold Whitby waves, while her hands were on the kite string making her a part of the wind and air.

"It is like fishing in the sky," she marvelled. "What am I fishing for? Dreams? Angels? Good spirits? It's so lovely!"

Energy was being drawn into her from the sky and from the ground. She thought of Benjamin Franklin flying kites in electrical storms and envied nobody. She thought, "I am perfectly all right now that I'm flying a pink kite with a rainbow tail. It's illogical and astonishing and wonderful. I am happy and sad and I will always be both. That's what it is to be me. To be this particular old woman who is connected to both joy and pain as the kite is connected to earth and air."

The pink kite in the blue sky lashed its rainbow tail and pulled its string and grey-haired Carole continued her dance between the green sea and the yellow sand until the red sun set.

Barbed Wire

"It's my land," said Lou, "I am putting up this fence".

"What for?" Hetty asked. "You've got no livestock on this section and the *piccanins* are paid to watch the sheep on the other side. Why spend the money?"

Lou didn't answer. He started to push the last splintery oversized wooden reel of jagged rusting wire towards the open end of the truck.

"*Fuga moto, you lazy kaffir!*" Lou yelled at the sweating man who was unloading the rough fencing stakes.

"Hey, Boss Boy!" He turned his attention to the only man apart from himself wearing a hat.

"Shift those bloody *skellums*. Get on with this job or I'll beat the whole damn lot of you tonight."

The labourers moved with reluctance under the ascendant sun. By sunset their legs would be cut and bleeding and they would have ripped their already minimal tattered shirts into bandages for their torn hands. Hetty shrugged and looked away. Lou mustn't see her eyes. He mustn't read her expression.

"Finished?" she asked, a moment later. Lou grunted as Hetty handed him the tin box of sandwiches and the whisky bottle of milky tea and sugar that she had prepared for him and insulated by carrying it inside an old woollen sock. He would be here all day alone with his '*boys*', though they would get nothing to eat.

Lou reached behind the driver's seat for his *sjambok*[1]. At the

---

1   Sjambok, a leather whip

sight of it his mongrel bitch made an inelegant scramble on her belly from beneath the truck to be out of his reach. She kept her eyes on Lou while scything the grass with her tail in an obsequious show of pleasure. The dog would spend the day with him on the anthill in the shade of the winterthorn tree.

An image of a solid tower of barbed wire and fencing stakes reaching a mile into the sky presented itself to Hetty. Inside the tower were the anthill, Lou and the dog. Outside it ten black men danced around shouting and jeering. Hetty dared not feel pleasure at the imagined scene. She allowed herself to feel pity for the dog alone.

"There's enough diesel to get to the store and enough dollars to buy rations and replace the diesel. Pick me up here at sunset. Don't forget to collect the herbicide to prepare the seedbeds, the rat poison for the storeroom, the arsenic for the termites and the medicine for my bad stomach," Lou said.

Hetty hoisted herself up into the driver's seat. The truck smelt of Lou, of the grease and sweat of his body. There was enough fuel to get the five miles to the store and enough money to return to the farm. The town was seventy miles south and Lou had almost finished putting barbed wire fences around the entire farm. In the quiet before the diesel engine turned over, Hetty heard him shout at the labourers and the cringing bitch.

"Anyone tries to desert from this farm and I'll *sjambok* the lot of you!"

Hetty used both hands to shift the gear into drive and both hands to let the brake off. The truck lurched forward, its engine grinding, and bumped away from the farm.

"I won't forget anything," Hetty told herself. "Herbicide for Lou's morning coffee, arsenic for his tea, rat-poison for his beer and brandy and the medicine for his bad stomach. I'm a good farmer's wife."

Fishing

Marie watches the bream as it follows her glittering spinner back to the boat. She has an instinct for the one that will take her lure. She knows which one will bite. She has a gift. She knows which fish's journey leads to the inevitable outcome of hook and net. Now she watches one particular fish rise to the surface. It grows in distinctiveness as it rises up through the thinning water. Marie sees the red spots on its fins, its round vacuous eyes, its mouth opening greedily. She thinks of George and how quickly and easily he took the bait, though she was the one rising up through the water.

George was a weighty catch but lacked stamina. Soft and rich he had been lounging by the pool in his impeccable slacks and blazer. Unable to take his eyes off her sleek snake-scaled swimsuit, he watched as she stood upright across the swimming pool. With careless grace Marie had dived in, her body lithe and undulating, her nipples pointing towards her quarry. She surfaced at his feet in one smooth movement. With eyes shut in faked oblivion and mouth open in contrived ecstasy, she sent a glittering line of shaken droplets curling past his nose. He was hooked at once and she had him safe with one swift scoop of her landing net.

"I *am* so sorry!" Marie had said. "I've splashed you – let me give you my towel."

Marie sits on George's new turbo-jet speed boat on the Zambezi. His present of the most expensive Abu Garcia spinning reel rubs against the large diamond solitaire on her left hand and pinches the fat of her palm. Marie thinks viciously what a clumsy oaf George is as he jerks himself upright in his golf shoes and tries to untangle his line. The boat rocks uneasily. He turns to Marie for help. She turns and smiles at Barry. Agile Barry steps over her feet to help George. Barry is George's golf club friend, an expert fisherman and their guide on this first trip down the river. Marie eyes Barry's neat butt and muscled legs. His voice is as deep as the river under the boat but his conversation lacks the sparkle of the water.

Marie feels the knock of a fish on her rod, the immense satisfaction of the sudden pull, the weight of an acrobatic creature as it tugs against her hand.

Fish are deft creatures perfectly made for their environment. They can only be caught by trickery and landed with skill. Marie despairs of George. He's no fisherman. He isn't a sport. It took no skill at all to catch him and already he bores her senseless. Marie watches the river from behind her Gucci shades. She sees trapped air bubbles rise up and burst through the surface of the water. Inexorable as sex and death, she thinks. A surfacing fish appears to grow rapidly in size. Its first appearance is indistinct. No matter what colour the fish, it will seem pale and glowing as the greenish water flows downwards over it. Human bodies have the same pallid colouration as they twist upwards from the bottom of a river until they pop up, bloated with gas. Men float face down. Women float belly up. Like dead fish.

Marie casts her line again and the silver spinner races, sparkling, back to the boat, desperate to be out of danger. At the last moment a fish swirls round to descend back into the murk, swift as a lead weight. That's the moment a big tiger-fish strikes. Hard and fast. Its teeth are knives at the heavy end of a curved muscle of rainbows. If you hook one it will fight to be free like a jet-propelled bulldog. Sometimes a small crocodile, attracted by the thrashing of the water, will follow the tiger-fish inwards, towards the boat. Crocodiles rise to the surface as fish do, but their approach is slower, deadlier, without compassion. Infinitely more dangerous. Marie yawns and thinks of sunburnt bodies twisting together in a bed and of George in the teeth of a crocodile.

Anything is possible on the Zambezi River.

The White and Black Blues

I'm inside the wrong skin. The idea strikes me while Dad is boozing at the Ruzawi Clubhouse bar and I'm killing time with Ted under the shade of a lucky-bean tree. Ted is seriously annoying me.

"Your Dad's a waste of white skin," he says.

He flicks his cigarette next to my bare toes and watches my expression as he grinds the stub into the red dust. No way could I rescue that *stompie*[2] to share with my *shamwari*[3], Patrick.

"You're a total waste, you drip!" he adds.

Ted had been Dad's farm assistant until he took him on in a shouting match. Bad call. Dad is a champion shouter. He can outlast a thunderstorm and still shower you with spittle. Dad gives Ted the sack and ferries him to the clubhouse so he can cadge a lift back to the city.

Dad isn't much good as a farmer, but does the colour of his skin matter? Most of his visible bits aren't white. They are the sour lemon yellow of the first leaves of the tobacco harvest. The edges of him, fingers, teeth and face, are the rusty brown of the last tobacco leaves that his black labourers pick by hand. Dad doesn't need much skin. He's a little bloke with a chesty cough and wire coat-hangers for shoulders that bend around a shirt pocket rigid with cigarettes.

My mate Patrick's father, The Reverend Nkole, is the opposite in size and colour to Dad. He's a pastor in the Tribal Trust land where Patrick goes to the local mission school. At weekends Patrick does odd jobs and skivvies for the Ruzawi club manager. I'm here in case my Dad gets plastered and I have to drive him home. I'm too young to have a licence but I drive our car anyway. Patrick can't swim, play tennis or even come into the clubhouse because he's an African. I can swim if I want but there are usually only little kids and their mums at the pool and that embarrasses me.

If you're Rhodesian, it's obviously better to have a white skin, but how can skin be wasted on anyone? It pretty much fits unless you are so old that it's loose and scraggy. My Mum's skin is soft and sags. When she's tired she's flat as a burst balloon. I personally don't have skin to spare. Like Dad I am short, bony and sharp-featured. My skin is brown, with scabs on my knees and bruises on my arms. I don't think my skin is me, though – like – did I choose it? If I cut my skin it hurts and bleeds. One of our workers ripped the skin off his leg on a ploughshare. He yelled, but my Dad swore at him and he went quiet. I stared at the blood running over his foot and between his toes. Underneath his dusty black skin his flesh was the same pinkish-red colour as mine is when I graze my knees.

Ted gets a lift to town with a farmer who needs to buy spare parts. He chucks his bag into the back of the truck, clambers in and goes without saying *tot-siens*[4]. I wander into the clubhouse. Dad isn't leaving any time soon and Patrick is busy scooping leaves from the swimming pool. An old piano, lid open, stands by the platform that serves as a stage. I tap at the keys softly. One or two just clack, a few others sound wrong. We don't listen to music at home. Mum has forgotten how to play Beethoven's 'Für Elise'. Dad has a record of something he calls 'Swing' by Harry James, which I mustn't touch. At boarding school in the free hour after prep, students sometimes bash out a mad version of Chopsticks. It sounds great. I would love to play the piano but no way will I admit that to anyone, and especially not to Dad.

---

4   Au revoir

Dad's in a bad mood because of drink and the fact Ted has gone. He shouts at me for the first half of the drive home. I'm a waste of space, he says. I always wasted time, he says. I tell him what Ted said about him. Of course, he slams on the brakes and tells me I can bloody walk the five miles home. He clouts me across my ear for "good measure", something he often says when thrashing me.

I hate Dad. I hate Ted. I don't know about me inside and my skin outside yet – when I do – it will be my secret.

I wait for the car's dust trail to settle before I follow. It's still very hot and I'm majorly thirsty but I daren't hang about. It gets dark really fast in the bush. Though the farmers say they've shot all the lions, you never know for sure and leopards are extra sneaky animals and appear just where you don't expect them. I am still in a rage when the sky turns grey. I have goose pimples and a prickly feeling down my back when I hear a car behind me. I'm not sure whether to hide. It would be humiliating to explain why I've been dumped on the road. From the racket the car makes I reckon that it's a crappy old banger and probably belongs to a local African. Africans can sometimes be really kind, especially to kids, so I stand up and look hopeful. It won't do to arrive back home too soon but I can wait in the tractor shed till I judge it's about the time it would have taken me to walk there. The car stops, my friend Patrick waves out of the window and his father, The Reverend Nkole, climbs out and wraps me in thick tweed-covered arms. Now I'm ashamed because I suss that the dust from Dad's car is smeared on my face with my tears and boys my age aren't supposed to cry.

"Dad's punishing me," I explain when Reverend Nkole offers me a lift.

The Reverend considers.

"I'm visiting the workers at the next farm. We'll drop you home afterwards."

At the farm compound there is a celebration going on and the Reverend blesses everyone. The women bring orange squash and bread buns for the Reverend and give some to me as well, though not to Patrick. I suppose it's because I'm white that I count the same as the Reverend to them for food, but it feels wrong. Patrick and I are the same under our skin after all, so I share my food with him.

I begin to feel happy. The workers clap their hands, sway their bodies and stamp their feet in rhythm to the drumming. Everyone sings. Everyone knows how to fit their voices together in different ways that match, even when their voices are higher or lower than each other. I don't know how to describe what they do or how they do it but I can hear that it's simple, and easy, complicated and right. I begin trying to rock my body and shuffle my feet along with everyone there.

Patrick says, "White people can't sing and dance like us Africans."

It's true that white people don't sing and dance as they work.

"Watch me," I say.

We laugh and together start to stick our bums out and slap our feet onto the soft dirt in a sound and rhythmic pattern.

———

My father has given me a helluva problem. His name is Jim Waller so my name is Tom Waller. It's an ordinary name but that doesn't stop my mates giving me grief about it. At boarding school when we're supposed to be asleep, we listen to the Hit Parade on a radio smuggled in by a rich, posh student. We're motivated to keep up with the latest tunes. One night "Honeysuckle Rose" is on the list, even though the guy who sings it has been dead for years. I think it's a pretty cool song and so do the other boys at first. The dead guy's name is Fats Waller and he is black. I don't know how anyone found that out because we can't buy records and hardly ever see pictures of the musicians. Too bad because it means I'm called either Fats Waller or Nigger Waller for the rest of the term.

It makes me really furious, though it takes me a while to work out why. I'm supposed to hate having the same name as a black man but instead I'm angry that the blokes think they're insulting me. It's odd that I feel that because where I live, white people act as if blacks are stupid and inferior. I can't think like that, because Patrick is my friend. I can also thank my Dad for my attitude. He had been in the war in Burma and fought alongside African soldiers. He's a stingy employer and brutal, but in a weird way has respect for his workers.

"They're brave men," he says and gives me another mean look.

Dad has a new ginger-haired farm assistant from England who is really friendly. Mum smiles at him a lot. His name is Pete. One evening he asks me if I like jazz.

"What's jazz?" I ask back.

Pete laughs. "Come and listen," he says. "I've got a new record of a mega jazz pianist called Oscar Peterson."

Pete lives in a *rondavel,* a round thatched hut, behind our farmhouse. He shows me the photo of Peterson on the record sleeve. Peterson's black like Fats Waller. I realise that white people and black people can like and play the same music. I remember that The Reverend Nkole has told me his brother, Moses, plays in a band in town.

Pete tells me about jazz, where it has come from, how many different kinds of jazz there are, how it's always changing and how it all started way back in Africa and came back to us after the slaves of America had changed it. I know something about that because one of the farmers says that the Civil Rights movement in America is unsettling the Africans in the cities and it's just as well that his farm blacks are uneducated.

I like the Oscar Peterson music. It reminds me of Fats Waller and "Honeysuckle Rose" so I tell Pete about Moses, The Reverend Nkole's brother.

"He plays in a dance band at a hotel. Patrick says that sometimes other musicians come and play with him after hours –

even white ones – it's called jamming or something."

"That'll be jazz," Pete nods.

At the farmhouse my Dad gives me another clout across my head.

"If you spend your evenings listening to music with a bloke, people will say you're a bloody fairy," he says. "Get yourself a girlfriend."

I don't ask Dad what a fairy is. One of the boys at school tells me that fairies are poofters, not real blokes. They do things with men that are forbidden by the Bible. When I hear this I feel sick and giddy same as I did when I was a titchy little kid and hid in my mum's wardrobe among all her slippery scented frocks. Girls' clothes are so different to boys. If a boy's voice isn't broken and he can sing, he might get chosen to act a girl in the school play and wear a skirt. Apparently, that gives you the same bad reputation as fagging for a prefect does. I don't understand why. Anyway, I cheek the English teacher and make the older boys laugh at my jokes so I never get picked.

I want a girlfriend because it sounds interesting, but I don't know any girls. The boys at school pretend to be offhand about dating but you can see the idea makes them jumpy. Some of them claim they've had loads of birds. Boys at school talk about rugby, balls, sex, girls and willies. Patrick is a lot cruder about that stuff, but in his own language and I don't have English words for what he says. As for the three white girls at the Ruzawi clubhouse, I can't fancy them. They're younger than me but taller and fatter. One has little tits. They don't fancy me either. They say so to my face.

———

For some reason my parents worry about me. Mum has started to watch me behind my back, if you know what I mean. I can't grasp Dad's attitude to Mum. He seems to feel a futile rage about her. I've seen him in the same helpless fury when the tobacco barn caught fire and when our old dog was strangled in a wire noose trap. I suss that he takes it out on me because he doesn't think I'm going to be much use to Mum.

After the Fats Waller name calling, I bunk off from boarding school on Saturday evenings. Some boys bunk off to prove they're hard mega-cool blokes. They hang around the flea-pit cinema, smoke marijuana, and get into fights with the poor white boys from across the rail line. When I bunk off, the blokes think I'm tough. I let them think that, but it's not true. I'm too short and skinny to risk a fist fight and too scared of getting hurt. I know what it's like to be hit. Instead I go to meet Patrick and his Uncle Moses at the Queen's Hotel in the run-down part of town where the white bums live. The hotel bar is dead cool. Patrick and I make ourselves useful behind the counter washing beer glasses. I get to know all the drunks in town and say hello to them in the station waiting room when I take the train home at the end of term. They fake that they are also waiting for a train.

Weekends, after the dinner dance finishes, Moses and his band play ace jazz till morning. I think that's normal for a hotel until the police turn up and shut the place down because Africans are being served spirits and it's after hours. Mostly the police leave it alone though, and pay informers to tell them if politics are discussed at the bar. The hotel is a seriously mixed up place. Blacks and whites drink together in the bar. Indians come and Coloured guys too. There are some very pretty black and brown girls in shiny dresses with loads of lipstick who sit at corner tables. Patrick rolls his eyes when I ask about them, but he knows all their names. There're two blokes there who I think might be poofters but nobody seems to care so I don't ask.

The whites who go to the Queen's Hotel aren't like the parents of my schoolmates. There's Ian who is a bricklayer from Glasgow. He came to Africa when Africans weren't allowed to be bricklayers. Then, as he said, he got lucky with his own construction business. He prefers to hang out with Africans because they play football and like jazz. He plays the trumpet when Moses and his band are having a jam session. I get to know one helluva lot about jazz and jazz musicians from him and Moses. Ian explains to me how the musicians take it in turn to catch the music and then develop it in a way that only they can do with their particular instrument and maybe every time it's done in a new and different way so the jazz is always moving and living like life and like the African drumming on the farm.

"People are like that too, Tom," Ian says. "Look at me coming to live in Africa. We are always in transition – nothing is fixed in the world."

One evening I think my end has come and I'll be expelled because when I arrive in the bar a teacher from school is there.

"Waller," he says, "What are you doing here?"

"I'm on an Exeat, Sir!" I reply, thinking fast. I smile at the brown girl hanging onto his arm.

"Hello Shupi," I say to her.

I reckon he won't report me.

After that when I jerk off, I think of Shupi and what it is like for her to have sex with my teacher.

I love the Queen's Hotel bar. No one either bothers me or minds about me. Nobody notices me. Patrick thinks it's rude to stare into another person's eyes but he glances sideways at me.

"Africans call white people *"muzungus"* – it means ghosts – you're a ghost Tom – you keep yourself secret. Maybe there's a spirit inside you waiting to come and terrify everybody."

I'm chuffed at the idea that I have no substance and am a hidden danger but I throw a wet dish cloth at Patrick and tell him no one is able to see him in the dark.

———

The most fantastic thing happens.

Satchmo, the great Louis Armstrong, the best jazz horn player ever, comes to Southern Africa. So, for sure we want to see him. Practically the whole bar and Moses' band from the Queen's

Hotel plan to go to the Showground for his concert. There's a bad moment when we're told it will be cancelled because the whites plan to have one concert for themselves and a separate one for Africans. Satchmo says no to that.

"I ain't gonna perform for no segregated audience." The band at the Queen's Hotel cheers. Imagine a black guy telling whites where to get off!

The dignitaries in suits have to arrange to fix up the Showground stadium for Satchmo instead of the Drill Hall in the city. The white ladies in hats, coats, gloves and handbags have to endure the dark and cold. They get seats while we – all the black guys and me – stand, but we're happy just to be there.

Satchmo sings, Satchmo scats, Satchmo plays Fats Waller songs – my songs now – Satchmo plays the trumpet. I'm the most thrilled I've ever been in all my life. Satchmo and Velma Middleton sing. Satchmo plays "Skokiaan" as a trumpet solo and the audience goes wild. That's an African song written by a friend of Moses, August Musarugwa.

I want to be a jazz musician. Jazz makes my heart swell up and ache but I have to admit I'll never be a performer. Patrick is miles better than me at singing and dancing. At least I've the grades to go to university. I might be a teacher. Why then, do I feel so bad and so sore? What am I really inside of me?

I think myself pretty smart bunking off on Saturdays but it's good for me in other ways too. I cover my tracks by being a Grade A in class and even get made a sub-prefect. I'm not tall enough to be a full prefect. The other students think I'm a big deal because I'm so wasted on Sundays from lack of sleep that they're convinced I must have been on drugs and had sex the night before. I even get myself a girlfriend. Miriam is okay but we don't really have the hots for each other, we just pretend that to make the other students think we know about sex. As well as jazz, the bar of the Queen's Hotel is a place for political arguments so it's easy for me to impress Miriam with my opinions. She tells me how Hitler and the Nazis banned jazz because it was the music of 'niggers and Yids'. She says she personally likes jazz but her parents only listen to classical.

We talk about our plans for university.

"You have to go to 'varsity." Miriam says, "otherwise you'll be conscripted and have to fight Africans in the bush war. That means you'll have to kill Patrick."

I know that. I'm not going to kill Patrick, but Patrick doesn't have the same choices as me. Patrick wants to go to University in Uganda but he has been told by the African National Congress to go for military training in China. People with black skins have started to fight people with white skins for their rights. I won't have my life and friendships decided by my skin colour. I definitely decide not to join the army. For once Dad agrees with me.

"Nothing will make you a man," he says, "but a war in this country will be bad for everybody."

That's a moderate comment from him. He's more relaxed now I have a girlfriend, even if she is Jewish. Then, at about the same time, everybody's lives change. Miriam goes to Israel with her family. Some of the jazz musicians get fed up with the police harassment and go to London. A surprising number of my schoolmates emigrate to escape being drafted into the army. After I'm awarded my degree, I leave Africa and move to London to escape conscription. It means I can't go home two years later when my Dad dies of lung-cancer. Twenty years pass before I cry for him. It takes me that long and two children before I understand that he had loved me. Mum sells the farm within a year of his death and moves into a cottage in town with her sister. I have no idea what happens to Patrick. The only place from my youth that carries on unchanged for decades is the Queen's Hotel. Moses stops playing there but other black jazz musicians take over. I want to believe that the music and the mixing carry on because listening to live jazz and seeing real musicians seems to have ended for me.

———

Jazz in Britain is nothing like jazz at the Queen's Hotel. Ninety-nine percent of British people have no interest in jazz at all. It's Beatles, Beatles, Beatles and the Stones. Of course, I think they're fantastic and music and dancing stay a big part of my life like the anti-Apartheid Movement and the anti-Vietnam War demonstrations, but that essential bit of grit and glory is missing. The mad mixed-up-ness, the misery and the magic mood are not part of Rock and Roll as they are part of jazz. The only skins in my life are the ones in which I roll marijuana.

Jane and I meet on an anti-Apartheid march. She finds my African stories authentic and assumes I am too. We get married. Everyone does. On our winter honeymoon we go to Paris and spend a whole night in the Jazz Caves of Paris. It's so dark and smoky down there that I carry no visual memories away from the experience; only the sounds and a return to the intense power of the live and living music. Jane tells me that the American jazz musicians, Dave Brubeck and Nina Simone, each had a classical music education but racism had forced Nina to leave for France where black jazz musicians are loved and admired. I tell Jane that Hugh Masekela and Moses Nkole have found England less welcoming than America.

London has surprisingly few jazz venues. There's Ronnie Scott's Club in Soho. It's interesting but you have to pay to go and drink to stay there. I go once or twice to the New Merlin's Cave in Clerkenwell but jazz is only played on a Sunday and that's when I take my kids to Hampstead Heath. There's jazz on telly but it's surrounded by too many personalities and too much talk. I make frequent visits to Doug Dobell's on Charing Cross Road and build a collection of Jazz Greats on vinyl. I buy all the old black American blues singers, Satchmo, of course, Billie Holliday and Ella Fitzgerald. My British collection includes Kenny Ball, Acker Bilk, Ken Colyer, George Melly, Lonnie Donegan, Chris Barber, Ottilie Patterson and Humphrey Lyttelton. They're good. I love their music. I especially love Ottilie but none of it's the same as listening to live jazz at the

Queen's Hotel. The jazz musicians themselves are mostly white and well-educated. They don't have the neediness, the drive, the passion, the energy of the black musicians back in Africa. There's no pain and no displacement. It doesn't get under my skin in the same way. Perhaps my skin is impervious because skin colour seems to matter less here? Certainly I don't feel so wrong inside. The secret and desperate desire that I couldn't define isn't bothering me right now.

I'm a long-haired English teacher at a comprehensive in Islington; Jane is a social worker in Camden. We're both great believers in hopeful outcomes and social progress. I'm too busy to question myself. Boarding-school and life on my Dad's farm means I'm tough enough not to have discipline problems with the kids I teach in spite of my short stature. Jane and I see eye to eye literally. I joke that being the same height makes us better sexual partners and that you have to be the same height to attempt the Kama Sutra. Naturally Jane is all for Gay and Lesbian Rights. I am too. I march with Jane for Women's Liberation. My daughter and my son can expect a future of gender equality. I discover women and femaleness for the first time in my life. I learn how women are constructed by biology, created by society, and survive through their own logic and dynamics. I'm busy and happy and in love with my practical and generous Jane and our two children. Life measures from okay to very good but my alpha male African upbringing remains an undigested boiled sweet stuck in my oesophagus. Somewhere I am blocked.

Jazz in Britain is static but the pop stars metamorphose into extraordinary, off-the-wall beings. They become androgynous and thrusting like Alice Cooper and David Bowie or wild, desirous and gay like Boy George and Freddy Mercury. They're exciting, their music arouses me but I'm not like them and don't want to be. Luscious drag queens strut provocatively. A man turns himself into a blonde Barbie doll called April. None of it makes sense but it disturbs me. There's an incident of homophobic bullying at my school. I try to address the issues with discussions about Shakespearean cross-dressing and Greek heroes who loved each other.

Time passes. Our kids become teenagers. One day the family watch an old TV programme about jazz musicians that features Satchmo and Fats Waller.

"Yuck!" my daughter, Tamara says, "Why do they pull those gross faces when they play?"

"They had to grin and be stupid because that's how white people wanted them to be," Tristan, her know-it-all brother, answers. I'm silent. It hits me like a smack in the face that I too, am pretending. I'm a fake, a face-puller whose instinct for self-preservation is a habit and a deception.

Who am I deceiving? Me? Jane?

Our kids go to university.

I'm head of the English Department. Jane is a senior social welfare officer. Our mortgage is minimal and our house has quadrupled in value. Jane and I have two silent empty bedrooms. A new hollowness swells up inside me. I feel off-balance and confused. Jane says it's time for a haircut and a new style. I need my long hair, however. When I'm alone I flick it forward to hide my face as Miriam once did. Then I take a curl of hair in my mouth and cuddle my balls and penis in my hands while I try to work out the relationship between my head, my heart, my genitals and me. Desire and the sexual act seem to be outside the conundrum that is Tom Waller. How and why and who am I? Do I want to know? Dare I tell?

————

I dream of walking down dirt roads in Africa terrified of leopards, unable to call out for help. Patrick comes towards me with a smile and my heart leaps.

"Tomi!" Patrick says, adding the affectionate African extra vowel sound to my name. "Marry me, Tomi!"

Overcome with happiness, I flick back my hair now as rich

and dark as Miriam's and hold out my arms. With the immediacy common to dreams, Patrick changes into a horrified Jane whose face runs with tears. My nightmares keep Jane awake for several weeks. She frowns at me.

"What's wrong – is this an identity crisis?" she asks, intuitive as usual.

I shake my head.

"I'm mad," I tell Jane. "I can't be a husband – I'm not a man. I'm really a woman."

Jane laughs, chokes, then becomes still and quiet.

"Sort yourself out, Tom."

"I don't know what I am," I plead. "I'm me – but I am not male."

I'm lying. I've always known what I am. I kept it a secret even from myself.

As usual we take our annual family camping holiday in South-West France. Afterwards Tristan departs for Istanbul with a friend and Tamara travels home via art galleries in Paris. Jane and I journey to the village of Marciac to a huge jazz festival; a musical caravanserai conjured up in the French countryside every August at the inspiration of Wynton Marsalis, the black American jazz trumpeter. It is intended as a second honeymoon for Jane and me in a jazz heaven with live music, wine, tapas, and foie gras. Instead, the excitement and amplification of live jazz after such a long fast turn me inside out. The dangerous spirit that Patrick had seen hidden in me frees itself. I tell Jane that I am other – not a man. I inflict terrible wounds on her heart and soul. Our holiday becomes a blue, black and bloody hell. Each night Jane and I scream at each other and weep. Every morning we hold hands and struggle into the crowded village square to get drunk at a new bar.

"Why did you hide this from me?" Jane says in distress. "I could have borne it otherwise."

Jane and I are equally shocked and equally unsurprised by my admission of my gender dysfunction but I have been treacherous. I ruined love. I wrecked everything by living a lie.

"Are you going to do it completely, Tom?" Jane grimaces making an involuntary downward gesture in the direction of my groin.

"I don't know," I reply. "I don't think this is really about just my penis."

"A keepsake – to remind you of your wife and kids?" she says with bitterness.

I crumple, blinking away more tears.

"I don't love you with my penis, Jane. I just love you and the kids!"

"And what will the kids feel?" Jane screams. "You've hidden your true self from them!"

I spend a month away from home, then Jane and I talk. We go to Relate for counselling. I see a therapist and a medical consultant. Finally, we tell our children what's going on. They're decent kids but they would prefer a conventional divorce. We have conversations where they don't look me in the face. We have unfinished discussions that are really about themselves and their discomfort.

"What kind of woman are you going to be?" Tamara asks.

"Are you still my Dad in a dress?"

"I don't know how this works yet," I tell her.

I start to cry so Tamara walks off. Kids hate that stuff from their parents.

Tristan says "Are you a hermaphrodite? Were you born wrong inside with missing – um – parts?"

"According to the doctors we are both normal – I have male gonads and Jane has female gonads. It's not about how I'm made physically it's about how my mind and soul are and feel. I am not the way men are expected to be."

"Why didn't you tell us all this long ago?" my son asks.

It's too complicated to explain the past when I don't even know how to live now.

When we recover some equilibrium, Jane tells me about a transsexual bass player and jazz composer.

51

"She's a very ordinary sort of person, Tom – apart from the music she plays and writes."

"Sounds like my sort of person," I say. "Thanks."

We manage to smile at each other.

"Was I a disappointment as a lover?" I ask Jane when I move out.

"You were kind and generous – that matters. I might have liked more sexual domination," she replies. "How about me, Tom?"

"You were – are – loving and true," I say.

Can I survive in the open without hiding, without secrets?

———

Nowadays before I leave home I check my appearance in a mirror. I see a middle-class, fifty-plus school teacher. Some things haven't changed much but my heart still jumps under my small round breasts when I look at me. That's me – the real me – now – exposed at last. I have long hair fastened up, conventional clothes, and thin pink lips. I am a very ordinary person who follows jazz festivals and writes reviews and articles for small jazz magazines. I am happy. There is live music under my woman's skin at last.

Dany and I met at the Deuragon Arms in London's East End.

The landlord of the Deuragon Arms is a jazz enthusiast and a Drag Queen. He hosts occasional strip shows but compères jazz performances as "Dusty Springfield". It's all rather shambolic and amateurish but it's another mixed up place where I can go without attracting attention and it isn't a heated gay pick-up joint like most Soho bars. I'm comfortable enough to be Tomi at work and in private but still need practise with social life. I wasn't looking for a partner but none of us stop hoping for romance. When Dany spoke to me, I noticed his South African accent and the attractive way his grey hair contrasts with his brown skin. Dany has a warm slow smile.

"Are you here for the jazz or the weird people?" I say, then curse my over-sensitivity.

"Both," he says, "Listening to soul, hoping for a soul mate as weird as me."

"So that's two of us, then," I joke. "Perhaps we had better just talk about jazz? Tell me about you and jazz."

"First place I listened to jazz was at Dizzy's Dive in Cape Town before District Six was finally destroyed by apartheid. I always wanted to play jazz." Dany answers my question. "If I'm asked, I play guitar and do session singing for local TV or theatre. Don't earn my living that way though."

"So how do you survive? Write novels I suppose?" I take another long shot. Dany grins at my lucky guess.

"I'm busy with my third novel – another work in progress."

"I'm a work in progress," I say, "Like any piece of jazz music I'm in transition."

Dany nods. "Aren't we all like that one way or another – being human isn't that fixed for anyone? I reckon my Pa and Ma swapped sexes as they got older. Ma got a beard and Pa got tits – they used to joke about it to each other. They even got used to Zackie, my brother. He's a "moffie" – that's Cape slang for "hermaphrodite" or a homosexual – Zackie is a transvestite though – he likes to dress in women's clothes."

"You dress well too," Dany says, with appreciation.

"Thanks." I feel both shy and proud. "I model myself on the older Ottilie Patterson – with a tailored dress and a neat chignon. To be realistic – I'd never look like Billie Holiday even if I was younger."

We both laugh. Under our different skins we are as alike as two drops of water yet, as jazz plays with time and rhythm, we are transforming ourselves and each other. I tell Dany I have secrets.

"Everybody has secrets," Dany says. "We know each other through love and skin contact and we still have secrets."

"I'm planning to go to the Montreux Jazz Festival this year", I tell Dany.

"Me, too", Dany says, smiling. "How about we get together when we're there?"

"Sounds good" I answer, hoping.

Mrs. Chicken

Though I have been alive about half a century, I contain several millennia of knowledge. I have experiences that range from animal sacrifice and divination, to sciences not yet documented. As an innocent child of five years old I was sent out into the farmyard to collect eggs. There I was brutally savaged.

I did not see my assailant. He came up behind me. I remember a great whoosh of feathers across my shoulders, and then he struck repeatedly at my bare legs with a sharp weapon. I remember panic, other people shouting, the stickiness of crushed eggshells, and running away.

We sat down for our Sunday roast next day. It was a time when grown-ups were so tall that I never spoke to them.

"Did you like your food?" Father asked.

I nodded, looking at his shirt button above the table.

"We have just eaten the big fighting cock that attacked you," he said.

The pleasurable intensity of my revenge rather shocked me but as there were neither feathers, claws nor a beak on my plate I knew the monster had actually escaped. Aggression does not reduce to white meat and gravy.

I liked our chickens. Lifting their hot, heavy bodies off the nest and collecting their smooth warm eggs was satisfying, even while they blinked and clucked in protest. There was safety too, in their friendly busyness and gossipy scratching in the dust in our yard. I liked to sit on the high concrete step by the back door to

55

watch our kitchen boy kill chickens for the table. I was no longer the victim of primeval force for whom justice had required a medieval sacrifice. I was a scientist working from first principles, like Leonardo da Vinci.

Our chickens did not run around headless because the kitchen boy gripped their bodies when he cut through their necks. It wasn't the inevitable deaths of our chickens that I found interesting but their extraordinary warm and smelly insides. I experienced tremendous excitement when I discovered that I could identify a red heart, shiny liver, spongy pink lungs, a muscular stomach, and know that, apart from a crop full of grit, my interior was made the same way. Most curious of all was the folded, twisted multi-coloured intestine. I poked my finger into its soft moist coils and at once divined my mortality. It was like, and was not like, the bruised pink snake the kitchen boy had killed by the chicken run.

"Snake steals eggs," he said. "Chicken kills snakes."

My second-hand National Geographic magazine had a photograph of an eagle with a dead snake in its claws. The eye of the eagle and the eye of the snake were hard and bright and functional.

I was old enough to help Father and Mother with their chores. Father made me stack copper coins into twelves and twenty-fours. Next it was my job to tilt the rocking, slidey, piles sideways and wrap them into neat, white paper columns for the bank. Mother made me wipe the eggs clean with a damp, grey rag, weigh them on egg-cup scales, and sort them into small, medium, and large sizes. Together we loaded them onto cardboard trays and packed the trays into wooden paraffin boxes for her customers. The grime from the coins was harder to wash off my fingers and smelt worse than the chicken shit.

Mother invested in a new deep litter system of raising poultry for eggs. The chickens were crowded together in a courtyard thick with straw and shit. When a broody hen stopped laying and refused to leave her eggs, she was suspended in a wire mesh cage until she lost all desire to be a mother of chicks.

We had a new neighbour.

"Make him welcome," Father told Mother. "Show him around."

Our new neighbour had a hard, black, bright eye. He also sniffed a long dry sniff very similar to the hiss of a snake. He was impressed with Mother's poultry sheds and even more with her customers. Six months later Mother came home looking tired. She told Father that her customers had abandoned her for our neighbour who had completed the building of four brand-new deep litter poultry units.

"You shouldn't have shown him around," said Father.

———

I married a young man who was a dairy farmer and smelt of cheese. After our honeymoon he altered his business plan and changed his stock from cows to chickens. He decided to go into the factory farming of poultry. He had several barns of battery hens and the same number of pits of chicken shit. His bank account bulged with money. The chickens, however, had crumpled legs, bald patches, cropped beaks and shut their eyes against the constant daylight of their brief lives.

"Don't you pity them?" I asked my husband.

"Aren't you lucky!" he said, "All you have to do is take care of me and the kids."

"It's a horrid way to treat hens," I said.

"It's nothing to do with you," he said.

"The farm stinks," I said.

"Watch what you say!" he said.

My husband smelt of metallic grime instead of cheese or chicken shit.

I won praise for my children and prizes for my flower garden. I had the most productive vegetable beds in the district. Plants grow well on bountiful chicken shit and water. My friends said I had made a veritable Garden of Eden. I was no Eve, however.

My breasts were too plump, my hair too soft and feathery. My husband employed a secretary to help him with the farm accounts. She had shiny, stockinged legs and a sleek, undulating body. As the office was near the battery farm, she had to make use of a large bottle of entrancing perfume. My husband was swayed and their eyes locked. I considered the time-honoured practice of voodoo to deter them but it seemed a shame to behead a handsome cockerel and hang it up to bleed outside their office. I knew that my husband was used to dead battery hens so I did not consider stringing up any of those. Only for a moment did I entertain the idea of burning down the battery sheds.

Now that I am older and alone, I have a small garden. I keep a few fat hens and a bantam cockerel. Long ago, when humans changed from hunter-gatherers to farmers, and from wandering in the forest to working on the earth, women and chickens joined together for their mutual benefit. It is still so today. Whenever I get out my giant claw of a garden fork, my hens run under my feet to tidy up the turned earth and remove any insects. They seem to count me as a one-legged member of their flock. At night I shut them away from danger. In spring I shut my seedlings away from their chicks. Every morning I eat a new laid egg. Sometimes I eat a chicken.

There is one thing that still remains true. When my hens roam freely around my plot, snakes keep away.

The Will to Love

When Agnes' heart burst, an earthquake tore through the fault lines in her family, splitting them apart.

At first, they did not realise what had happened.

The initial shock of her death flung them into the temporary shelter of a small hotel. Together they teetered on the brink of the chasm in which her coffin lay, clinging to each other for support. They looked gravely into each other's tear-stained eyes and said that it had brought them closer together and re-established family ties.

They lied.

The ground under their feet was trembling and the final cataclysm of Agnes' funeral would complete the destruction. The next time they were together on the same land mass it would be for another family funeral.

As the low buzz of Mr Hoskins' voice read out her mother's Last Will and Testament, Emmy felt the presence of Tamsin. She no longer thought of Tamsin every wakeful second of her life but only at those times when she was still or alone. Since Agnes' abrupt death last Sunday, she had been too busy to think of her own daughter. There had been too much to arrange, too much to plan. She had to make the cheap funeral worthy of her mother. She had to manoeuvre the loving drunken friends and the mostly sober relatives into different spaces so they didn't offend each other. She had to watch her sister Annie all the time in case she drank herself beyond mere numbness into a coma. Emmy didn't have Tamsin's address but Tamsin wouldn't attend her grandmother's funeral because she, Emmy, would be there. Only one grandchild, Annie's son, Seth, would be at Agnes' graveside.

Emmy's sister-in-law was expected from Canada but her brother had been killed in a car crash fifteen years before without ever having had children. Emmy's family had failed as parents. Either they had not had children or they had rejected or neglected them. It was a fact, not self-recrimination. If there was a contract between parents and children then she and Annie had failed as children too. Emmy felt unemotional about it. For the moment she had stopped punishing herself over Tamsin and Agnes, but neither did she allow herself the indulgent dream that one day she would be reconciled with Tamsin. Whatever else anyone might claim, parenting owed as much to luck and money as it did to good intentions and hard work. There was always the chance element of the child itself. Or was it the rogue element? How else could you explain the difference between two siblings like herself and Annie? Or the difference between cousins like Seth and Tamsin. Even if virtue and courage were inherited, they weren't dished out in equal amounts.

Death, duty, money, property, will. The words kept taking turns to surface in her head so that another word eluded her. Was it perhaps, Love? Over-exploited, under-used Love. Was Love an emotion, an instinct, a duty, a need, a genetic imprint? A dull despair had settled on her chest like a heavy cat when she looked at Agnes' dead face in the morgue. She had expected to feel the sharpness of bereavement, a swelling sense of love and loss, but she only felt tired as she and Annie looked at the exhausted painful grimace worn by her mother.

At the sight of her mother, tears flooded Annie's face like rainwater over a weir. Emmy saw the mortuary attendant fidget and glance at his mops. She dug out more wadded tissues.

"We failed her." Annie wept.

Emmy tightened her mouth and her grip on Annie.

"We did not!" she thought, fierce and defensive.

"We didn't succeed in helping her – that's different! Agnes had lots of friends," she said.

She thought of Agnes' lovers and carousing partners. They could always be counted on to stay till the last bottle was empty.

"She had plenty of love. We loved her, Annie, you and me and her grandchildren."

It was a mistake. Emmy hunted for more swabs as Annie keened louder.

"I've lost my only child. Seth doesn't love me any more. It's his father's fault. It's not fair. I wasn't like you. You drove Tamsin away."

Emmy hunched her shoulders against the deluge. She had learnt not to flinch at the idea. She knew it was her responsibility that Tamsin had gone.

The word 'will' conjured you up in my head at once. In your silent, unsmiling way you were a wilful child. You willed yourself not to give in to your mother, to your teachers, or to anyone, not even to make your own life easier. You willed yourself not to forgive.

You were a precious bundle. Your tight hands and face squeezed shut; your small curled body compressed into the white swaddling blankets that hospitals provide. Because you were nearly prevented from being born you were doubly prized. You fought so hard to live after your mother had to give up, unconscious after a wrongly administered dose of pethidine. You continued battling past any mere need to survive. You still battle on, your eyes shut, fighting off friend and foe indiscriminately. At least your heart must be unbroken otherwise you would have given up as Annie is preparing to do. As Agnes' heart has done; worn too thin by an excess of grief and alcohol so that it finally ruptured.

You are a precious child still even at the full five-foot ten stretch of your lovely lanky body. Are you happy without family nearby to love you? Have you found someone yet to prize your unique beauty? What are you really doing? Fighting for love or fighting it off?

Mr Hoskins' voice was a wasp trapped in a beer bottle as he read the formal words of the will. Emmy's mind was occupied

61

with Tamsin. The family had known the contents of the will years ago. Agnes had never had any claim on her husband's estate and he had never had any control over it. It would have been entailed away from Agnes to her son if he had lived. Now it would eventually revert back to the Crown because even Seth, the only surviving male in the family, was excluded by being descended from a daughter. During her lifetime, Agnes had been granted a small living allowance if she did not marry again. It was enough to keep her in drink and lovers. It wasn't really a living allowance thought Emmy. More of a dependency allowance. Enough to keep her hooked. Enough to keep the family on tenterhooks.

Emmy fancied that the three women in her family, Agnes, Annie and Tamsin, were sitting in a row next to Mr Hoskins. They turned an intense stare towards her. Three pairs of blue eyes under straight dark eyebrows, Agnes' face like crumpled white ostrich-skin, Annie's soft, pink-rouged and flaccid, Tamsin's sun-smooth ice-cream. Her own face, the mirror of theirs, was sharp and sallow. Emmy thought that all four people were unknowable, mysterious, even to themselves. Their physical family resemblance may have been marked but it was impossible to unravel the delicate intricacy of the character differences that marked them as separate individuals or the confusing tangle of needs and affections that linked them.

The drone of Mr Hoskins' voice had sounded after the death of Emmy and Annie's father thirty years earlier. Emmy had managed then to understand what her mother could not explain years later, that Agnes was disabled and damaged by being reduced to a mere dependent. Listening to Hoskins again, Emmy felt that her ribs were collapsing into the vacuum left by the shrinkage of her heart. She had felt the same at fifteen as she watched Agnes, already a prisoner of grief and alcohol, made even more helpless by an outdated system of inheritance.

"You have nothing to worry about," Mr Hoskins had said. "You are provided for, provided ..."

Provided.

At the sight of Seth, Emmy's heart made a bungee leap into the abyss then jerked back into her empty chest with an elastic thud. He was another version of Tamsin.

"Hi, Auntie Em – I mean Emmy." Seth was awkward for a moment. His father encouraged him to be formal but he knew Emmy disliked being called aunt.

"I'm sorry, Emmy. I miss Grandma too." He gave her a long hug in his usual spontaneous way. Emmy's eyes stung. He smelt both strong and vulnerable. His arms and shoulders felt firm and light. Tamsin would feel the same. He was crying unselfconscious tears and Emmy loved him for it.

"Tamsin?" Seth was looking at her. She shrugged, made her smile clownish. Seth understood.

"Mum?" he asked in code. Emmy rocked her head in a yes-no, no-yes, so-so way. This time Seth pulled the clown's face. Emmy knew Seth worried about his mother but she had encouraged him to obey his father and not get involved in Annie's frequent rehabilitations. Her support for Agnes while Tamsin was growing up had cost too much. Emmy wished again that Seth would break all the family traditions by being happy. She watched him return to Annie and stand for a long while with his arms around her while his mother sobbed and sobbed.

Once the funeral service was over, Emmy acknowledged that she had been watching out for Tamsin all through it. The left side of her ached with the effort of not twisting round at the expectation of Tamsin's voice. She had wept helplessly as the chief mourners rose one by one to speak of Agnes though she couldn't tell whom she cried for most, Agnes, Tamsin, Annie, Seth or herself. At least she had managed not to be incoherent when it came to her turn. She had planned what she would say with care. It had occupied her thoughts most nights for years past.

"I don't know what Love is," she said. "I don't know if Love can ever be managed right. Perhaps Agnes wasn't careful with Love, perhaps Love wasn't careful with Agnes, but Agnes had courage and never gave up on Love. I guess that sometimes Love is not convenient or appropriate, I do know that Agnes was always loving."

Emmy looked at Seth. She thought how sometimes Love has to absent itself from what it finds dearest, though by doing so it does not negate itself.

She would find a space to say so to him afterwards. Now her head was occupied by her conversation with Tamsin.

You are a war zone, a no man's land; a place where contracts cannot be made and do not hold. Either you do not understand the significance of a pact or you have dispensed with conditions. Sometimes you seem to be proud and independent. Sometimes you seem to be a feral creature, both vulnerable and dangerous but outside the law. As a child you set up a temporary base camp at home but you always meant to desert it for a more defensible place remote from the family that threatened your integrity. Who could blame you? You saw Love as the bait in the trap. Love was the drugged food that weakened resistance. Curious then that you stayed to continue the fight for so long. Perhaps you were afraid that you would be tracked down and recaptured so instinct made you determined to leave no trail behind you. Not only did you immediately kill any new-born love but you ate it. In the end you had to be driven out for your own safety. You had to be shown the open door of the cage and beyond it, the road to freedom.

Yet you still had to be told to go.

Annie was no longer crying. She was quiet, her eyes blind, focussed inside herself. Emmy, looking at Annie, wondered when she had given up and how much longer she would go on.

"It is better not to feel; to have nothing at my heart. Mother is dead but I feel that I never had a mother. Seth has left me but I feel that I never was a mother to him. Emmy does not love me. She can't love. Even her daughter has run away from her."

"I have not got the balance right between needing love and giving love. There is a black hole inside me that is swallowing me. I can do nothing. I have no future."

"I cannot bear Mother's death. I cannot bear my life. I don't have a protective skin and everyone eats away at me. Seth, my beloved son, is here by my side but he doesn't care about me. He cared for his Grandmother. He won't come to see me again now she's dead. It's unendurable. His father has told him lies about me. His father wasn't kind. He wouldn't help me through my bad times – so like a man not to care for those in need."

"Change yourself," he said. "Don't be like your mother."

"How could I do that alone? Mother was always with some new man or other. She thought of herself first. She needed love like I do. If only Father hadn't died. It was different for Emmy. She despises weakness. Look at how she treated Mother. Look at how she treated Tamsin. I'm vulnerable. Agnes and me are not survivors."

"I feel nauseous, my head hurts terribly. I need a painkiller on top of my Valium. There's only tea afterwards. That's not right. Agnes would have hated that. What about her friends, she'd ask?"

"Perhaps her friends will bring their own drinks like I have …"

"Seth isn't staying tonight. I know it's to avoid me. His father has told him to say it's because of exams but it's not. God, I've struggled. I'm frail physically; in and out of hospitals. I always help other people, but they let me down. Either they are hopeless drunks or they are the hard sort and they desert me when they're well. The world's cruel. It's against my nature. I cannot bear to be unloved. I need a drink – just one drink."

The first solid thud of earth hitting the hollow shell of a coffin then rattling into pieces has a terrible finality. Seth went white with the shock of hearing it for the first time. Emmy, holding Seth's arm, managed not to cry out. Annie, on Seth's other arm stooped closer, transfixed. Her hand closed on a lump of earth holding it tight. She gently laid it in her coat pocket. Tonight she would pillow her cheek on it to sleep. The chasm in the earth was closing up but the ground was tilting away. By nightfall they would all have separated and gone to distant places. There would be no coming back until the next funeral.

"Tamsin I love you," called Emmy as the ghost of Agnes slid quietly into the night.

Disappearing Woman

The Camp staff were busy before dawn. They worked so quietly that the first sound the guests heard was a clonk and slosh as a bucket of hot, clean water was placed outside their tent with the diffident greeting, "*Muli Bwanji*[5]. Safari is ready."

By sunrise the fishing safari had departed purposefully downstream. The noisy outboard roared and failed twice before finally igniting. It chugged out in reverse and then screamed away briefly before settling into a steady throb that could still be heard in the distance a good twenty minutes later. Ann stayed in bed with her eyes shut, listening to the shushing sound of its wake in the reeds below the tent. Andy and Paul, her husband and son, were going bream-fishing above the rapids some fifteen kilometres away and she had no one but herself to consider for a whole day. With a feeling of pleasurable indulgence, she had decided to stay in bed half an hour longer and not even to go on a game viewing trip. Once the water had settled back into its brightening smoothness, she got up and began to dress slowly, timing herself so she would be ready when she heard the sound of the Land Cruiser leaving. The departure of the game-viewing safari was somewhat drawn out. Piet and John had massive hangovers, the result of drinking two crates of beer each the day before, and were bad-tempered and slow. Ann could just about hear their affable wives' high-pitched discussion. They were deciding which route to choose in search of the pride of lion that had been hunting upriver the night before.

Finally, the sound and dust of the Land Cruiser faded and the silence was overwhelming. A dense, total absence of sound. Ann's skin prickled deliciously with fearful pleasure at her complete solitude. Gradually the sounds of the bush re-established their dominance and her ears began to distinguish from the mingled sounds those of river, birdsong, insects, small creatures and the shifting, rustling growing abundance of vegetation. Longing to absorb the wildness of the bush into herself and to nourish herself with its variety and self-sufficiency, she wandered up the river bank as far from the busy hum from the camp kitchen as possible. Half a mile or so up the river bank she would still be quite safe provided she checked for hippo returning to the water after a night grazing in the *dambo*[6]. Nobody had seen elephant or lion close by for a week and the hyena had been heard far away across the river.

Once the camp was left behind, Ann had to admit that she was grateful to be neither expected or needed on either action-packed, exciting safari. Previously she would have gone fishing with Andy, partly to enjoy the adventure and beauty of the river, partly to make sure Paul survived his initiation into manhood activities by his father. Recently she had become aware of Paul's need to distance himself from her. At seventeen he definitely considered himself grown enough not to need her protection and he showed it by putting on an air of tolerant patronage of his mother that infuriated her, while escaping Andy's notice.

"A great deal of family feelings and behaviour escape Andy's notice," Ann thought, frowning. She wondered how and when his indifference had come about and her movements momentarily slowed.

Ann's skin, hair and bush clothes were variously browned or bleached to the subtle colours of veld grass in winter. She had cool brownish hair with sunny streaks, a pale, but sallow skin,

---

6   A shallow wetland

except for hands and knees that were inevitably browner than the rest of her.

"I sort-of blend into the bush," she had joked to her kids. In fact, her eyes, which she described as the colour of a muddy African river, actually had green sunlight in them and her lively expression and quick bird-like manner made her appearance ineffective as camouflage. Ann would joke that she was neither one thing or another. Neither thin or fat, blonde or brunette, tall or short, pretty or plain.

"Not fish or fowl, fool or famous, Madonna or madam," she grumbled to herself, mockingly repeating a family joke. Then determinedly quickening her step, she made herself concentrate on her surroundings.

Ann found herself a thick patch of green grass under a waterberry tree where the bank rose steeply above the river. She looked round carefully for signs of danger and then hunkered down comfortably with her binoculars. On her last visit she had spent an absorbing morning watching six elephants slowly cross the river upwind of her and browse on the floodplain opposite. Today she sighed as she glanced round. She had a feeling of unease, of something forgotten or unseen, a sense of the proximity of a predator. Something was waiting out there, watching her with malevolent, lidded eyes.

"Nonsense," she told herself. "So often the bush is just – empty – except for birds and small, secret creatures and crocodiles, of course, in the river."

Looking at her feet in their comfortable *veldschoens*[7] and socks, Ann remembered last night's fireside stories. Some English youth out to work at the camp had found the heat unbearable and refused to believe that the unbroken surface of the river hid crocodiles. All they found of him was his canvas tackies[8] on the sand by the water, then later an arm wearing his watch in the

---

7   Ankleboots
8   Plimsolls

belly of a huge croc. Ann thought idly of her *veldschoens* placed neatly side by side on the river bank with the rolled socks tucked tidily into the right one and herself nowhere to be seen. The idea pleased her enormously, and shocked her terribly.

"Why on earth, though?" she mused.

Suddenly, as if on cue at her thoughts, Ann felt the earth move with a cataclysmic shudder and her breath left her lungs in a harsh gasp. She felt a huge and solid weight strike her body and force her head downwards, but the ground underneath her was disappearing. It lurched sickeningly away and she fell on and on into a whirling abyss. Ann was spinning in space. Together, with the game park and the all the animals, she had become an infinitesimal dot suspended in a vast and infinite void.

Millions of years later, it seemed, Ann heard rapid breathing as if someone had been running and running. It was her own self panting. Amazingly, she was still under the waterberry tree. The river continued to glide past, gently concealing secrets and crocodiles. Nothing had changed. Outwardly she was intact, inside her guts were liquid as the water and much more troubled. Common sense made her consider explanations. The churning in her stomach was not from last night's excellent venison. Flying did not make her sick. The thought of a pair of socks and shoes abandoned on a river bank and her own absence had turned her world upside down. Appalled and shaken, Ann realised that she wanted to run away. While the Game Park had been whirling in space, she had decided, apparently without reason or motive, to leave Andy.

Last night they had gone to sleep a couple married for twenty-five years. Now she wanted to disappear.

"No one will know why! When I run away no one will know my reasons. No one! No one knows me! No one at all! I might as well not exist! I don't exist!" Ann said to herself in a rising panic.

The decision to go had been made apparently without any intermediate debate with herself. Almost, she felt, without her knowledge and yet with her complete consent. Already she felt that turning back was not an option and the choice of staying had gone a while ago.

"I am planning to do a 'runner'", she whispered, testing the ridiculous words.

"To run for my life like a duiker[9]." And she felt more foolish.

The weekends at camps in the bush were an established part of Ann and Andy's life in Africa. Andy, a high-powered Director of Operations, worked long hours and was often out of the country at conferences. Ann gave all the time she could spare from her role as company wife to a voluntary charity. She was an excellent manager and loved her work in spite of its frustrations but the bush trips had become essential for both of them to renew the energy they needed to face the challenges of living in a developing country. It was an opportunity to spend time together and for Andy and the children to interact away from the stress and socialising associated with his job. Ann told herself that they had a worthwhile life. Both had job-satisfaction. That was some compensation for having sent the children away to boarding school.

Each visit to the wild was an adventure. A journey to an experience based on completely different values to their daily lives. To Ann it seemed more real, more dangerous, but astonishingly, it offered more family intimacy. The drive to the tented camp was long and difficult. There was no electricity there, but good food was served and the bar was well-stocked. There was hot water for showers from the Rhodesian boilers by each tent – a forty-four gallon drum on its side above a fire. As there was no telephone Andy couldn't be contacted about the work that he left so reluctantly. His position gave him power and responsibility and both were addictive. He enjoyed decision-making and his fairness made him respected, but even in the bush he needed to be in control. Rather than watch game quietly, Andy preferred the thrill of negotiating the difficult river and the constant activity

---

9   A small antelope

of spinning for bream or pike, or fighting with the heavy river *vundu*[10] for his bait and its life.

Ann's passions were for birds and trees and walking in the bush and she had felt especially impatient for this particular weekend. It was curious, but over the last year or so she had a faint, though steadily increasing, sense of loss. A displacement had taken place in her world that she could not identify. She found herself distracted at odd times, standing in her living room, yet filled with a longing to be returning home. Ann would shake herself, putting it down to the need to escape to the bush.

"My need to touch base!" she would mutter and move off to check on dinner in the kitchen. After years of practice her home ran smoothly.

"Almost by itself," she said, but was secretly furious when Andy implied that it did.

"No one gives the "madam" any credit." She laughed, but didn't find it funny.

"I'm not just a housekeeper," she said defensively, but felt uneasily that something important was going unrecognised.

It wasn't satisfactory to know that though her excellent dinner parties may have eased Andy's business deals, the memory of them faded faster than the smell of the guests' *Romeo y Julieta* cigars. The three children also seemed less substantial because they were away so much. Paul in his final year at boarding school, Sarah at university in England and Lisa working for the first time in London.

Mr. Phiri, the cook, had become distant with years and efficiency. Fifteen years before, he had started in the garden doing piece work, then helped with cleaning and laundry until he graduated to culinary skills. His status, regular salary and perks gave him a position of importance in his own extended family but in spite of everything Ann did, she felt he regarded her with even more disdainful mistrust than when he had first arrived and

_____
10   A catfish

72

expected to be arbitrarily sacked at any moment. Ann could only smile wryly.

Once she said. "Mr. Phiri knows me best of all my family!' Then she was appalled by the significance of her own words. Whether it was while sitting above the river or while whirling in space, somehow Ann found that she had had time to review her whole life.

"I've had a near-death experience – like hell I have!" Ann said, trying to mock herself back into some normality, but life seemed both very precious and completely altered. Ann found she wanted to hold onto the epiphany of her ride in space even while her terror increased with every moment.

The sound of drums announcing mid-morning breakfast and the return of the Land Cruiser party came distantly to Ann's ear and she got stiffly to her feet, compelled to return to human company and to try to forget her new obsession.

"It's just menopausal nonsense!" Ann berated herself, rubbing a crick in her back. There could be no reason for leaving Andy. He was a good provider, a pillar of society, faithful probably, even at his conferences abroad. Ann was sure she loved him. She frowned as she tried to measure how much.

"After all this time – of course I love him."

"Does he love me?"

She was surprised to feel indifferent to Andy's love for her. It was as if she had gone past some marker in her life without noticing. Run some race alone so that winning didn't matter.

Mid-morning breakfast was in the grand tradition of bush camp meals. Fruit, cereal and a huge plate of fried egg and bacon with home-made bread inadequately toasted on the top of the wood stove. Andy and Paul would not return till evening, but Ann's other companions were jubilant with their successful game-viewing. Hangovers and tempers forgotten, they had spent the morning watching two lionesses and several cubs on a kill while the gorged male lions lolled in the grass, their limp paws as innocent as velvet cushions.

73

Piet and John were business associates of Andy's and regarded him as a good mate. They treated Ann with a slightly reverent, old-fashioned courtesy which Ann felt was because of Andy's position, but was really due to their South African upbringing. Ann knew them from years of attending the same social functions, amateur theatre productions, and school meetings. They were pleasant company, but not close friends. This morning they were carrying on last night's joke about the big fish dinner that Andy and Paul had promised to catch.

"Ja!" said Piet. "They'll buy silver fish from the village at Lubungo! Has Paul got enough money to pay for them? Man! He had better bring supper. I will be hungry tonight!"

"Oh you, Piet!" said Hattie, his wife. "You only ever eat steak!"

"How are the girls?" she said, turning to Ann. "Coming home in June?"

"Oh – probably I will go over to England and see them this time," said Ann.

The idea of going on home leave to see her daughters only occurring to her as she spoke; what a simple way to arrange the start of a disappearance!

"Don't you get scared on the river bank by yourself?" said John's wife, Noreen.

"Ja, Annie!" said John patting Noreen on her bottom. "If I was Andy, I wouldn't let a little thing like you go without a boy to watch out for you."

"Hey, Cecil," he said, turning to their camp host, Cecil Pretorius, "You should send a game guard with Annie here."

Cecil, tolerant of guests who spent a lot of money at his bar, winked at Ann.

"Annie's tough, you know. When she is tired of Andy, she is coming to work for me as a safari guide!"

Ann smiled, relaxing with their mild concern and flirtatiousness. Both she and the wives knew it was meaningless, especially at breakfast. The men wanted to go and get their first beers and they wanted everyone happy before they did. As they rose from the table Ann felt her stomach heave. A feeling of indigestion, or was it something that had not been said. Something about Andy was nagging her! It was true that he didn't often express any concern for her.

After breakfast Cecil Pretorius guided Noreen, Hattie and Ann on a walking safari. Noreen jumped at grasshoppers but Hattie's knowledge of birds rivalled Cecil's and Ann was deeply content once more. The shared interest of them all was companionable and the walk was wonderful. They came unexpectedly on a family of giraffe. Ann felt that of all wild creatures, they were the most remarkable in appearance and the most extraordinary in their natural state, neither threatening or threatened. They watched without speaking for a long time.

Ann avoided any futile small talk until they gathered in the bar before lunch. Then the chat was about servants' wages, the state of the economy and the role of Andy's company in liberalising currency transactions. Ann felt the pressure of her daily life again and her stomach knotted. During the conversation she found herself being asked what Andy thought. It was a common situation for her. Luckily lunch was a sleepy affair with everyone looking forward to dozing through the white heat of the afternoon; the men in the bar, the women in their tents.

The heat was indescribable. Ann could never recall exactly the quality and intensity of a hot bush afternoon when she was back at home. Once it pressed her down under its yellow, prickly, weight, she didn't know how she could ever forget it. It forced her into accepting the hostility of the place, so harsh, so full of life, so full of death, and with a total disregard for her existence. Ann was not sentimental about the wild. She felt liberated by the concentration on survival it required of its creatures. Free to let odd thoughts trickle through her mind as her body sweated and itched.

"*I* need to survive.! – Good God! – *Me* in danger! – Why do I feel that I am at risk somehow?"

"Is it work?" Twisting on the camp bed to avoid the slant of a scorching sun shaft, Ann knew her job was coming to an end and she must find something else to do.

"Is this why I feel restless?" she wondered.

Funding had been found to pay a salary for the job Ann had done voluntarily. Many applicants had had been listed, most more interested in the money than the work. Ann would be needed only to facilitate the handover.

"I can't bear to have no function other than running the house... but what to do?"

"Another voluntary job that I set up for someone else?"

Ann had told Andy she was to hand over her job. He wasn't especially interested. Occasionally it had inconvenienced him.

"Do you really want to work, Ann?" he asked. Then, seeing her expression, said quickly, "You'll easily find something else Ann – you are very competent – it's just – well – a lot of effort for no return."

Ann grimaced.

"I could get a really good admin job with a decent salary back home. I like to work and be independent. Actually, I wouldn't mind doing a course in Business Studies..."

"Oh well! That *is* impossible, Ann." Andy ended the conversation.

Ann thought now with a little lift of her spirits that it needn't be impossible. It would be fun to use her talents, to work for money and herself and just be Ann.

"Maybe I can learn again."

"I could do it. I could manage. I know I could."

After smoky-tasting camp tea, in the cooling afternoon, everyone set off downstream on the game viewing boat. The river sliding by was slick, green, and swift, still swollen with the last season's rain. Gazing at its surface, Ann was again overcome with panic. They planned to rendezvous with Andy and Paul and return in convoy at dusk. Ann felt that confusion and flight would be written all over her face. Andy would stare at her in irritation and turn away in scorn. To calm herself, she stationed herself where she could chat to Cecil as he slowly and lovingly swung his huge, flat boat past rocks and shallows and pods of hippo. From there she could see the riverbank. Malachite kingfishers darted through the shadows and great green and yellow crocodiles lay motionless on the sand of the east riverbank. The others were on the roof of the boat with beer and gin watching antelope on the floodplain.

"The game is not so good this year," said Cecil, shaking his head.

"The poachers are under control – not like last year, but this year we lost our best antelope to the game capture teams."

"We have more tourists in the country than elephants now and the tourists are a bloody liability!"

"Phew!" He whistled ironically. "Hell, man, I don't make money here because my airstrip is not good enough for tourists. Maybe I'll dig up my road too!"

Ann and Cecil laughed. Cecil's roads were barely passable in the dry season and he ran his camp to please himself anyway.

Ann said, "They cull antelope for meat, not conservation. There is no way that wild creatures can survive that sort of pressure from the urban population."

"Look here, Ann," said Cecil. "We are all a disappearing species – you, me, and the wildlife of Africa. We will all end up in zoos!" They laughed again at the thought of a zoo for Cecil but Ann felt that perhaps what was frightening her most was the possibility of an open cage door.

When the fishing boat appeared, Andy and Paul were relaxed and signalled a good catch with raised fists. Their mealie sacks of bream were flung onto the bigger boat for the boatman to clean for supper. Iced beers from the cool box were passed over in exchange. Ann was relieved that Paul's fledging maturity had survived the day. No doubt it was helped by a successful day's fishing. Andy was easy with his daughters who didn't share his interests and intolerant of his son who did. He was impatient with Paul's mistakes, but then his own father had not been kind.

"Hey, Mom! You must see my *vundu*!" called Paul, aglow with pride and sunburn. "It's bigger than Dad's."

Andy was already comparing record catches with Cecil. He greeted Ann briefly.

"Hi! Did you have a good day?" His smile was familiar and reassuring.

"Lovely, darling!" replied Ann. "Congratulations on your catch! Did you see anything interesting?"

That was it. Everything was normal. Ann felt her panic slip away, insubstantial and unreal to be replaced, surprisingly, with disappointment.

Cecil turned his lumbering big boat around and set off slowly for the camp. Andy and Paul, on John's advice determined to try one last bream hole before following. It was dark when Cecil manoeuvred into the bank and his guests clambered onto the mud. The camp radio was beginning to whistle and squeak in competition with the bats. Cecil looked at his watch as he hurried off to discuss camp business with his town base.

"Andy and Paul should have caught us up long ago," he said. "If they aren't back when this is over, I'll go and look for them."

"Thanks, Cecil," said Ann.

It was like Andy to stay too long on the river. Ann hoped it was just that and not engine trouble. She didn't allow herself to think about a hippo attack. She hesitated a moment on the river bank, now all aglimmer with fireflies, but could only hear hippo grunting and blowing in the distance.

"There's nothing to be done."

Nothing could change the past. Nothing could change Andy or herself or their relationship. Now she must wait anxiously for the safety of them both. Meanwhile she would shower.

Showering under the stars in the grass enclosure of a bush camp is a unique pleasure. The hot water sluicing down soothes sunburn, insect bites and weary muscles and keeps the cool night air away. Ann, delighting in the sensation, tried not to think of Paul and Andy in danger but resentment kept rising up inside her. Suddenly she was not afraid for them but furious with Andy.

"Bastard!" she thought, trembling with rage. "How dare he!" "How dare he use me this way!"

Ann saw that Andy considered his investment in her over. He need do no more for her. She had her children, her home, and her social position. She was going nowhere and needed only minimal maintenance. Like his company Mercedes, she was a credit to past shrewdness. Once a discerning investment, her depreciation was complete and she had been 'written off' the books. She continued to provide a service as reliable as the Mercedes. Housekeeping, caring for the children, and sex were the measure of her value and in that order. Ann, the person, was lost. The part of her that was unique, awkward, funny, different, that was herself, counted for nothing.

Ann saw that she had known this fact for a while and had refused to acknowledge it. Perhaps Andy did not realise what had happened to them as a couple. Certainly, he had done nothing to prevent it. He cared most about his work. Maybe all he had done was be professional to the exclusion of every other part of himself. Ann understood that on Andy's terms she would be easily replaceable when she left. She must eventually lose everything but she would not lose herself. Ann didn't even consider trying to win Andy back. It wasn't her nature to play the vamp. If Andy could not value love and loyalty given freely and generously, then she could not forgive or value him. Shivering in the shower in the battered camp towel, Ann knew that she had been fighting off pain for a very long time. She knew it would engulf her. She also knew she would survive and eventually be whole again. As Ann watched the last soap bubbles trickle away into the sand outside the shower, she knew she would leave Andy and she understood why.

As soon as she was dressed Ann returned to the river. Fear was again replacing her anger. Judging from the crackling of static at the bar, Cecil was still busy on the radio but two of his men were standing by the landing stage with paraffin lanterns. They turned to greet her.

"She is coming, Madam," one of them said, smiling.

Immediately Ann could hear the faint phut-phut of the outboard moving with caution down the dark river. Another twenty minutes of straining to see and hear and then the boat nosed into the shore. Paul leapt out, flinging the painter at Ann and hissing in fury.

"I hate Dad! Stupid fool! He takes such chances with hippo!"

"Aren't you going?" Ann started to remonstrate feebly, recognising he had been terribly afraid, but Paul was past her.

"I'm going to shower and pee!" he shouted and was gone.

She turned. "Andy," started Ann again, but she could see he was livid and tired so all she said was that she was glad he was safe.

"Paul is a pain. We had to wait for some hippo to move off before we could start back," said Andy. "He behaves so badly!" He had not seen his own son's fear, but Ann saw what she had refused to see before. For Andy, adult behaviour was behaviour that did not ever give way to emotion – not fear, not hope, not sorrow – and not love. She felt a sadness for Andy, but for herself something like release.

"Have a drink before you shower, Andy," she said, reaching to help with his fishing gear.

As they approached the bar, Cecil came out.

"Oh good! You're back, Andy. Everything okay?" He glanced swiftly at them, assessing the scene with a hunter's eye for something hidden, and then, judging that no major disaster had occurred, said, "Come to the radio, Andy. Message for you from the Company!"

Andy's organisation needed him to fly abroad for an important conference in twenty-four hours. They had arranged a small plane in to collect him the next day. Andy revived instantly. A good day's fishing today and successful dealing likely on Monday. Paul's behaviour was forgotten.

"Can you drive back to town on your own, Ann?" he asked, turning to his wife with an absent-minded attempt at solicitude.

"No problem, Andy," said Ann, answering with an African phrase. *"Hakuna Matata!*[11] Paul and I will be fine. Paul can drive the four-wheel on the dirt. He is good on the rough and John and Piet will be right behind if we get stuck."

"That's great, Ann!" Andy squeezed Ann's shoulder briefly, his mind already in the boardroom.

"So you're off to Jo'burg, Andy," said Cecil, pouring out double gins for his guests while they were still around to pay.

"Good luck!" he said, raising his glass to them all.

"Cheers! To your next visit to the bush."

"And you, Annie?" he said, clinking his glass against hers.

"When do you go on home leave?"

Ann smiled.

"Oh," she said gently. "I'll be disappearing very soon!"

---

11   Swahili, no problem

The Child Who Kept Her Mouth Shut

The child kept her mouth shut and did not smile in photos. When she daydreamed and her mouth fell open, her father tapped her under her chin.

"Careful, or you'll look like a half-wit," he said.

He meant it kindly. He kept his chin up and his top lip stiff. He was never rude or unkind to those he considered half-wits, though he would get very angry with employees who behaved like half-wits.

When she wasn't daydreaming, she made sure her mouth was shut because, though she was nine years old, she only had one front tooth. The other children in her class at school had sung to each other, "All I want for Christmas is my two front teeth!" Soon they all had two front teeth.

She would whisper, "All I want for Christmas is my other front tooth," but it did not appear.

Her baby teeth had all become loose one after another. They had wobbled in an interesting fashion when she pushed them with her tongue but they hung on by tiny red threads of flesh. Her mother had suggested using string.

"Tie one end to your tooth; tie the other end to the handle of an open door. Slam the door shut quickly. It won't hurt," she had smiled. It was her joke.

In the end all the little teeth had come out one by one, as easily as pearly orange pips. Only a couple had little black spots of decay. Each had to be treasured in her sticky palm, then it went into a spare matchbox for safe-keeping till bedtime. It would be carefully tucked under her pillow. Her father always forgot to give the tooth fairy the silver coin she needed to pay for the tooth and he had to hand it to the child at breakfast. Perhaps it was this casual neglect of the tooth fairy that prevented one of her front teeth from growing. All she knew was that if she smiled a grown-up would ask, "Ooh! What has happened to your front tooth?"

So she didn't smile and they simply said, "What a solemn child!"

Then she was ignored because solemn unresponsive children are dull.

At last her watchful mother took her to a dentist whose surgery was on the third floor of a dark building. To reach the surgery her mother shut them into an iron cage with doors that expanded, then clanged. It groaned all way up and squeaked faster all the way down. The dentist's room seemed to be all made of dark brown sagging leather with shiny lumps and bumps. Behind the white-coated dentist, there was a machine like a giant dissected spider's leg. In front of him was a metal tray with detached silver spider's fangs arranged on it. The dentist and her mother talked together for a time and then they both looked at her for a while. They put cheerful smiles on their faces. She even had a hard machine pushed into her mouth to take an x-ray. The dentist explained that she had an extra little tooth in her mouth and it had stopped her adult tooth from developing as it should.

"I will have to cut the extra one out," he said. "I will give you an injection, so you won't feel anything."

After the appointment with the dentist, the child's mother took her hand and they crossed over the road to the office of the Christian Science Practitioner. The Christian Science Practitioner was a nice lady with teacups and sugar cakes, neat hair wound into tiny curls, spectacles that squeezed her nose, clip-on china rose earrings and stockings full to bursting.

"It's mind over matter," she said. "If you have the right thoughts in your mind, you will feel no pain. I will pray for you."

The child, however, was very frightened and her mind did not win over the matter of the pain. The injection hurt and its numbing effect did not seem to last very long, but she sat very still while the tears ran down her cheeks and the blood ran down her chin. Her mother and the dentist didn't look cheerful at all.

The ordeal ended, of course, her mouth healed and the child put the matter out of her mind. One day when she and her father were in the town, a man in a bow-tie and tweed jacket came up and greeted them.

"Hello, how are you?" he said to her. He had a kind smile. The child had no idea who he was, but she did not smile at him because she still had no front tooth. Her father looked at her surprised.

"Don't you recognise your dentist?" he asked.

"No," she said, also surprised.

Two years later she was no longer a child, but a girl in her first year at boarding school. She still had no front tooth. She still kept her mouth closed. She even looked serious when she was daydreaming. Daydreaming meant that she was often last in the line for going to classes or even for going into meals. One day she was so late that all the other girls were seated at their supper tables when she stepped through the door. The teacher on duty was a plain, shapeless, almost young woman who could not remember what it was to be a child or to be happy.

"Stand up!" she ordered the girl. "How did you get to be so useless and toothless?"

The girl kept her mouth closed as her father and her life had taught her. She knew that no grown-up worth their salt should ever be rude or unkind to someone without a tooth. Besides, her missing tooth had begun to grow. She could feel its razor-sharp edge against her tongue and she knew that one day the spicy bite of revenge would be hers to savour.

Useful Martyrs
A Memoir

"If Mum had been there – if she had been killed?" My sister Clare asked. "What would you have done? What would you have thought?"

"I'd be absolutely bloody furious!" I said, not caring how callous I sounded. "I'd refuse to go to her funeral!"

Clare regarded me warily. Not for the first time.

"I feel a bit the same – well – not quite like you – but yes. If Mum had gone there after all we said to her."

Clare and I were together in Harare. It was new for us to agree about anything. For most of our lives we've avoided sharing how we feel with each other. Our lives in Zimbabwe and Zambia had taken us down different roads into countries who opposed each other politically and we were just beginning to find our way back to friendship.

"If a train is roaring down the track towards you – you don't lie down in front of it and claim the train's making you a martyr," I said, somehow hitting on a metaphor that worked for me. I always think of trains when I'm in Harare. I once took the school train from Harare to Marondera, and Marondera is the home of the born-again Christian community where my mother lived.

"You don't choose to be a martyr. Martyrdom chooses you. If you are a Christian it's your duty to save your life – it's not for God to do it because you've put yourself in danger."

I'm not an expert on theology and martyrdom but my mother's decision to live in a Christian community forced me to think about ethical choices and God.

It was only a matter of months earlier that Clare and I had argued with Mum because she said that a martyr's death might be God's calling for her.

"Mum – isn't your community becoming a bit of a cult? All this unquestioning obedience and subservience. Look what happened at Jonestown! All those people killing themselves with Kool-Aid – it served no purpose!"

Mum was upset and offended. "How can you say that about me – about us?"

I backtracked. "Okay Mum – I'm sorry – but it is dangerous to go there. This terrorist, Gayiguso, is a very serious threat. Over 50 white farmers have been killed by his rebels in Matabeleland. You shouldn't go down there to the New Adam's Farm – really!"

"God will take care of us," Mum said with what I saw as a smug smile.

I turned away to hide my irritation. Privately, I thought she was indulging in a wilful, romantic notion of self-glorification, but Mum's Christian community was at the height of a period of successful proselytising. Their membership had expanded and two new branches of their community had just moved into farms in Matabeleland.

"They've asked us to go there and give them support," Mum said with determination. "Remember my friend, Jean, who used to live here with me – she has been born again as Sarah. She wants me to go down to the New Adam's Farm and see how they're all doing."

Clare and I could only shrug and hope. We had no way of knowing how soon our warnings to Mum would prove accurate.

"It was the war, I suppose," I reasoned sadly with my husband when I finally returned home to Zambia. "Guns, death and religion all seem to work together. Everybody's born again in Zimbabwe – both black and white people. Who can blame them after what they went through in the liberation war?"

I'm part of a complicated family. The Zimbabwe liberation war that had separated us physically had ended in 1980 but our divided allegiances had not been discussed or resolved. During the 1970s my mother and sister continued to live in white-ruled Rhodesia while I moved to Zambia. Zambia had hosted Joshua Nkomo's Zimbabwe African People's Union (ZAPU) and the Zimbabwe People's Revolutionary Army (ZIPRA), its armed wing of freedom fighters from Matabeleland who had fought against white rule. In 1980, however, Rhodesia had become Zimbabwe under President Robert Mugabe. The complication was that Mugabe's Zimbabwe African National Union (ZANU) and the Zimbabwe African National Liberation Army (ZANLA), its armed wing of freedom fighters, had been supported by North Korea and China and had operated out of Mozambique. That meant that Nkomo and Mugabe were rivals for power after the inevitable end of white rule. After independence a civil war between the armies of these two political factions seemed likely. This danger appeared to have been resolved when President Mugabe made placatory speeches about national unity and peace at his inauguration. Everyone, including me, wanted peace and a prosperous Zimbabwe after the destructive war so, reassured by Mugabe's words, I allowed myself to feel hopeful and all kinds of enthusiastic people and missionaries poured into the country to help rebuild it.

As early as 1982, however, only two years after Mugabe became President of Zimbabwe, stories began to appear about dissident revolutionaries carrying out acts of terror in the South-West of Zimbabwe. Reputed to be funded from South Africa, their apparent intention was to destabilise Mugabe's rule by encouraging insurrection among the Ndebele of Matabeleland. Diplomats and journalists from both Britain and the United States asserted this was true. It was also confirmed by stories from white-ruled South Africa. What was deliberately and criminally played down was the growing number of Ndebele people who were being murdered. Without knowing for certain who was responsible, Clare and I knew that terrorists were systematically killing white farmers and that was why we told Mum not to risk a visit to her friends at New Adam's Farm.

Mum had always been a churchgoer and a Christian. Her life had been tough and she suffered personal tragedies that included the deaths of two infants and her second husband at the young age of 54. For as long as possible, Mum suppressed her grief, but eventually it became too much for her. Without intending to, in the expectation of more pain and sadness, she would hold her breath. That meant she often blacked out. By 1976 she was passing out so often that she was finally admitted to hospital.

"It's a brain tumour, they think – it may mean an emergency operation!" Clare said.

After many months and a series of tests the neurologist decided otherwise.

"It's panic," he diagnosed. "Breathe into a paper bag when you feel dizzy. You're hyper-ventilating."

To him, Mum was just a neurotic woman and psychotherapy was outside his field.

Mum needed to believe otherwise. In her opinion grief did not kill. Cancer did.

"When I told Mum that she didn't have a brain tumour she turned her face to the wall and wouldn't speak to me," Clare said.

Mum's Christian community had prayed by her bedside and Mum heard what they said to her.

"God has cured me," she said ecstatically and she sold her home and all her possessions and moved into the Marondera Christian community that had befriended and cared for her while she was ill.

Years later Mum was still there. Clare and I knew that Mum's born-again Christianity gave her love and hope. We could not, and would not want, in any case, to take that from her. For all Mum's charismatic religious faith, she was a capable and intelligent woman, with sound common sense. While that sometimes put her at odds with her Christian brothers and sisters, the pressure they put on her to conform usually triumphed. Fortunately, she was still able to feel fear and when she was afraid, she held her breath and fainted.

"I don't think I'm well enough to go to New Adam's Farm this weekend. I've been dizzy and falling over again," she said when I phoned her from Zambia. "Perhaps next weekend."

It was, however, the very next Thursday night, the 26th November, 1987, when eight white people at New Adam's Farm were murdered, including a six-week-old baby. They had lived without security fences or any means of defence. Only one young girl escaped by running away. The eight Christian missionaries had chosen to believe that God wanted them to stay on the farm and that they needn't seek safety in the town of Bulawayo. Another eight people, together with their children, on the nearby Olive Tree Farm had made the same decision and were also slaughtered. The killers did not use guns. They made the African workers watch as they maimed and killed with machetes. Afterwards they burnt the bodies. The decision to massacre peace-loving, and unarmed white Christian missionaries, among whom were Britons and Americans, was quite deliberate. The international press focused on this particular horror and the continuing unexplained and under-reported genocide of the Ndebele people slid into the background of the news from Zimbabwe.

My precious Mum was alive and safe in Marondera, but in a state of extreme shock.

"Thank God!" I said, livid with rage and despair and irony.

I tried not be drawn into the terror and the tragedy of it all. But, of course, I was. I had my own quarrels with God and my own need to forgive and be forgiven.

I knew from bitter experience of life in a Front-line state during the liberation war that governments needed to be questioned. Even while I had friends who I knew were pragmatic idealists, the same criticisms would apply to revolutionaries and freedom fighters. I'd never felt comfortable with the stories about South

African dissidents in Matabeleland, It just didn't ring true. Eventually, after 1987, and following the New Adam's Farm and Olive Tree Farm massacres, a counter narrative began to emerge that differed from the one Mugabe's regime put out. It was an even uglier story of genocide organised by Mugabe himself.

Steve Williams, a Zimbabwean artist and arts facilitator, visited Zambia a few years later. He was looking at the possibility of setting up an arts college for the Southern African Development Community. We met through my work in a Zambian art gallery and quickly established a rapport.

Steve had been the only white man to join ZAPU, Joshua Nkomo's freedom party, back in the '70s.

"It's too dangerous to talk about now," he said, but he did confirm the disturbing news about the murders of thousands of Ndebele people by President Mugabe's North Korean-trained Fifth Brigade in what was known as *Gukurahundi*, – *"the wind that sweeps away the chaff"*.

"Mugabe wants to destroy any possibility of Ndebele opposition to him and his Shona majority government. Gayiguso, the man who carried out the New Adam's Farm massacre, was supposed to have been arrested," Steve said. "He wasn't ever inside a prison. I gave art classes at the Ingutsheni Psychiatric hospital in Bulawayo – he came to a few of them but he didn't seem psychotic to me. Next I knew, he'd vanished. I'm sure Mugabe faked his arrest, then covered-up everything until he could disappear."

"It's true," Steve continued. "Mugabe staged the murders of the white farmers to draw attention away from his genocide of the Ndebele."

I wasn't surprised by Steve's words. Nobody who had lived through that time would have been. Even anger wasn't a useful emotion. The sick fury I felt wouldn't make the truth any more believable.

It was not until 1997, ten years later, that the Catholic Commission for Justice and Peace in Zimbabwe and the Legal Resources Foundation completed their comprehensive investigation into the genocide of the Ndebele people carried out by Mugabe's crack Fifth Brigade between 1980 and 1988. They said they had proof of at least 8,000 deaths. The actual figure is probably between 20,000 and 40,000. In spite of the bodies piled into wells and down mine shafts, in spite of the burnt homes, in spite of the mass graves, in spite of the spoken and video testimonies, and in spite of the thousands of missing people, President Robert Gabriel Mugabe remained in power until 2017. He has never been held to account for his proven crimes. It is an extraordinary irony that Robert Gabriel Mugabe was brought up in the Roman Catholic faith and educated at a Roman Catholic school.

Though my mother was safe, fate didn't let me forget the New Adam's Farm deaths.

By 1992 apartheid was coming to an end in South Africa. South Africans were looking to a new future that would involve business and not war with other African countries. That meant that my husband, Mike, a successful practitioner in primary medicine in Zambia, was courted by a professional organisation planning to set up a tertiary medical evacuation scheme to South Africa. We were wined and dined and flown off to the Kruger National Reserve where the cash tills sang louder than the birds and we, the prey of big business, were flattered and fattened for the kill. Back in Johannesburg, the organising entrepreneur, Paul Davis, invited us to spend the last night of our trip in his mansion.

"My wife's a lovely woman – she'll look after you," he said. "Can't be there myself, but we've a guest suite and staff, so it's no trouble at all."

Paul was right. His wife, Jo, was a very special person. She was a consultant doctor at the Baragwanath African Hospital, a kind, hard-working, progressive woman. The one night we spent in her home, however, was the first and last time we would see her.

We were taken to our guest suite, our suitcases carried in by the staff and were invited by Jo to come downstairs for drinks and dinner.

"My parents are here – visiting from Zimbabwe," Jo said.

"Great!" I responded. "Whereabouts in Zimbabwe? Harare, like my family?"

She shook her head. She was so welcoming we knew we could look forward to a convivial evening. My husband and I grinned at each other and wasted no time descending to the bright, well-appointed lounge and the promised gin and tonics.

It was not at all what we expected. Jo's grey-haired parents looked blindly round at us, glassy-eyed and abstracted. From their open mouths came almost soundless words. They seemed short of air and kept turning their heads in vague half circles as if they couldn't see each other and had been abandoned somewhere strange. The conversation faltered, hesitated and died. I turned to Jo for some explanation of was happening. She sighed uncomfortably then shifted decisively.

"I'm sorry," she said. "It's the anniversary of my sister, Gaynor's, death. She and her husband and baby were murdered on this night five years ago. It's a very difficult day for my parents."

Mike and I stared at each other, horrified. We offered awkward condolences, wondered whether any conversation was polite, asked Jo if we should tactfully leave. We understood why Paul had not come back to spend the night at his home with his wife and with us. I hated him for it.

"How terrible!" I said, not knowing what to say. "Whatever happened? I'm so sorry!"

The room was thick and dark with a dense, hopeless grief that made us all prisoners, clamped in our chairs.

Jo's mother bent her head and turned to the wall. Jo's father gulped for a little more air so he could speak.

"They were Christians living at the New Adam's Farm," he began. "We prayed with them," he continued. "We told them – God has a purpose for you all."

"Oh my God!" I blurted. "My mother – you must know my mother – she was supposed to be there that week – oh my God!"

Since that night I have carried around inside me a well of guilt. My presence there that night must have increased the punishing agony that Gaynor's family were suffering. Our visit wasn't planned to add to that. It was just chance. That thought in itself heightens the horror of the massacre at the New Adam's Farm. Had what Clare and I said to Mum stopped her from going there? What did save Mum? Her own well-judged fear? Mere chance? What had Gaynor's parents said to her? Would she have listened to them?

I try not to remember the pit of misery we fell into that night. I hope never to see again the grief and suffering we witnessed there. It's surreal that the convoluted twists of accidental fate took me close to the horror that only just missed striking right into the heart of my own family, but it gives me no insight into the workings of heaven or God. When I think of Jo's parents and her sister, I can find nothing to offer or to say that might give them consolation or hope. Perhaps their Christian faith has been able to help them? I hope so, for their sakes. I can't imagine that it would give me any comfort. I don't know who needs forgiveness and who needs to forgive. I don't know what I would have done, or felt, or endured if my mother had been at the New Adam's Farm with her friend, Sarah, and with Gaynor's family that night.

Outside the terrible murders of my mother's Christian friends there was another much greater genocide taking place. It isn't possible to measure the suffering or to compare the personal significance of these dreadful crimes. They are, however, related. The New Adam's Farm massacre was used by Robert Mugabe to distract international media attention away from his extermination of thousands of Ndebele people in order to secure his own power over his country. That was his purpose and the use to which he put the faith of the Christian believers of the New Adam's and Olive Tree Farms. They had to die to provide camouflage for him and the actions of his Fifth Brigade.

A Child at the Queen Victoria Library, Salisbury, Rhodesia 1954
(Harare, Zimbabwe)

The bare-boned cement steps shine
shoe-sole and servant-smooth.

At five o'clock the doors are shut
and the books close their eyes.

I wait my collection by car-parent.
Always late, and better never.

Thick cypress trees make hot shade
over jelly-bodied termites with acid jaws.

A book is a step I can stand on,
a Jacob's ladder I can climb.

A book is light-knight armour,
a torch in my bed tonight.

I sit on my bottom outside the library
scraped knees make a book table.

The librarian takes tea upstairs
in the town's only museum

next to the silk cup and saucer
made by frustrated Bombyx mori.

I am a child alone with my books,
the old building sulks behind me.

A book is a thick yellow brick,
a Dorothy road I will walk.

A book keeps me swimming,
a mermaid alive in the sea.

I stroke the worn book cover,
cloth-bound board, soft-cornered.

So many readers have breathed
the smell of its dry paper

The pocket for its card is empty,
and my name is safe in a box

Four weeks to read two books,
then they must be returned

Demolished, gone, replaced.
Goodbye Queen Victoria Library

I find you on my laptop screen,
a digital image in grainy grey

I feel the loose curved spine,
the dented pressed gold words.

Its smooth pages open flat,
a loose thread in their seam.

The back cover has a red-dirt runnel
made by hungry and illiterate ants

Next time I'll choose more stories
and once again be lost and found.

Concrete and glass wings swoop
and fly us onward to modernity.

Words floating in a web of clouds
are printed on the pages of my heart
* The silkworm

Acknowledgements

John Corley for all his work editing, referencing, advising and retyping the material for these short stories.

Maggie Hablous for her considered and thoughtful reading and comments on the memoirs and several of the stories. Geoff Holder Dupuy for advice on *The White and Black Blues*. Sally Cline for her inspirational teaching many years ago in Cambridge. Tia Azulay for always being ready to listen and talk about writing. Jeremy Thompson of Troubador Publishing for his helpfulness and advice.

I am indebted to my second cousin, Judge Charles J Waddington, for his professional help with the accuracy of my short memoir, *Not in Front of the Children*.

 Matador

For exclusive discounts on Matador titles,
sign up to our occasional newsletter at
troubador.co.uk/bookshop